MW01268445

ON THE CUSP OF IT ALL

TALES OF AGE AND OF AGING

PATRICK CONLEY

authorHOUSE®

AuthorHouse™
1663 Liberty Drive
Bloomington, IN 47403
www.authorhouse.com
Phone: 833-262-8899

Published by AuthorHouse 10/14/2024

ISBN: 979-8-8230-3436-4 (sc)
ISBN: 979-8-8230-3435-7 (hc)
ISBN: 979-8-8230-3437-1 (e)

Library of Congress Control Number: 2024920765

Print information available on the last page.

Any people depicted in stock imagery provided by Getty Images are models, and such images are being used for illustrative purposes only. Certain stock imagery © Getty Images.

This book is printed on acid-free paper.

A FOREWORD & A FOREWARNING

All characters in this collection of short stories are fictitious. Accordingly, anyone looking for resemblances to living or deceased persons will be disappointed. Fiction allows us to escape from reality and to retreat from the seeming chaos of our lives. All the while, though, these narratives tease us into believing that this world of letters is real—if only momentarily. However, if the characters and situations remain as flights of imagination, they may, perhaps, express some element of truth.

CONTENTS

EXCURSIONS

The late afternoon routine of the Smallette family remained just that—a "regular and customary course of procedure" so Mr. Smallette's dictionary, yellowing with age, stated.

The front door slammed shut with a bang, announcing the grand entrance of thirteen year old Tommy. He slung his backpack on the floor and strode over to the kitchen, striding hard at first but then quickly transitioning into subdued small, silent steps like a thief in the night. He was hoping to snatch one of the few remaining brownies that always tasted better when they were stolen, not given. However, spying his father seated in his customary chair, Tommy composed his face into the image of a pseudo-suave adolescent.

When Mr. Smallette asked him, "How was school today?" Tommy shrugged his shoulders and responded in a cliche of bored affectation. "Same old, same old." He eyed that one remaining brownie on the counter, pounced upon it and swallowed it in one gulp.

"Well, Tommy, you must have read something different. It's the start of a new term, right?"

"Yeah, Dad, sure," the ravenous schoolboy responded, all the while scanning the kitchen to see if any other delights—brownies, cookies, cake, pie, even Ding Dongs—had been bought to be grabbed and consumed in a single bite.

"So, what did you do in English class?" prodded the middle aged man.

"Oh, some weird short story by a guy named Walter Mystified or some weird name like that. I mean Walter—that's the same of a certified dork."

Mr. Smallette ground his teeth. His parents had named him Walter Anthony Smallette. He always hated the name "Walter" and rechristened himself "Tony" in a nodding reference to his middle name "Anthony."

Realizing that he had nothing to gain by dwelling on this topic, Walter, aka Tony, decided to switch to another subject. "How's algebra going?"

"It's fine," snapped back Tommy— even Walter knew that that expression, translated out of the adolescent dialect, meant, "Don't bother me, buzz off, leave me alone, you old, meddling grouch." Tommy raced upstairs, shouting "I've got soccer practice." Walter felt as if a steely hard icicle had pierced his innermost being. When Tommy was a preschooler, Walter had enjoyed kicking the ball around with his son. Then, when Tommy turned seven, he had coached his son's soccer team. In fact, he had coached Tommy's team for five years. The squad had earned its share of victories, but the city championship had eluded the team's grasp. They had reached the quarter finals, but that was the end. Then, when Tommy had turned twelve, the boy felt he had to move on to greener soccer fields that would prepare him for future athletic glory—or at least a city championship.Walter sat there, stewing in his own sense of failure.

Then, Jane, Walter's spouse of seventeen years, returned from work and blew through the front door of their modest but comfortable home. "Walter, did you pick up that dog food on your way home?" She asked, even though she had already ascertained the answer. Years of experience had taught her the essence of Walter's character.

"No," Walter replied meekly. "It just slipped my mind. But I did get dinner ready."

"I hope you didn't fix a meal for four because Tommy's team will be off getting pizza after practice. And, as for Paige, in her fifteen and a half year old mind, she was dieting—which for her means no regular meals, just a constant snacking except when she was playing soccer or swimming."

"She burns calories faster than she takes them in," Walter replied. "I wish we could." Then he reflected on his own middle-aged spread. "I guess I'm getting older but not wiser, just a bit heavier."

Jane, for that was her name—even though she loathed it—lightly kissed the forehead of her spouse of seventeen years. "Well, you can pick up the dog food and a few other items on this list while you're at it. Then at least you and I can sit down for a dinner even if no one else joins us."

"Yes, dear, that will work out." Walter knew better than to call his wife of seventeen years 'Jane.' He knew she hated her given name. He recalled her telling him over and over again just why she hated her own name. "When I was just a kid, my so-called friends would chant, 'Plain Jane' over and over again. I grew to hate my own name more than ever." So, out of deference to his wife, Walter never mentioned it. "Besides," he thought, "I'm not so fond myself of my own name."

Sensing an opportunity, fifteen year old Paige emerged from her bedroom and descended the stairs savagely like a hungry bear ravenously looking for food after a winter's long hibernation. However, she wasn't pursuing food. She had other appetites on her mind. "Dad, I heard that you were going to the store. It would be the perfect time for me to work on my driving. I'll be sixteen in a few months."

Walter swallowed long and hard. He recalled their first outing with the car. They drove in the local high school's parking lot on a Sunday morning. "It will be safe there," Walter had assumed. It wasn't. After a few leisurely spins around the lot, Paige spied the cones designating the practice area for parallel parking. "You're doing great, Paige, so far." Why he said that mystified Walter. Paige stopped the car well enough in front of the forward cones. Then she put the car in reverse and floored it. The wheels spun, Walter gasped and then screamed, "Stop, Stop." Paige didn't hear her father's frantic screams. She had put her her ear plugs in and listened to her favorite band, Death & Destruction . "Stop, Stop." She did. Then Paige drove forward and annihilated the forward cone.

"That was easy," Paige determined.

Walter fumed, and huffed and puffed and got out of the car in a rage. "Where are the cones? Where are they?" He repeated over and over. Then he got down on all fours and, peering underneath the car, found them embracing rear and front axles.

"Dad, what are you doing?" Paige queried out of shame and embarrassment over her father making a spectacle of himself—even though no one else was within eyeshot. "I mean I parked the car, didn't I?" Then, as a mark of the seriousness of the situation, she took the ear buds out and said again, this time, more angry than alarmed, "Dad, just what are you doing?"

Walter rose from his prone stance, gritted his teeth, and did all he could do to stop from shouting. "Here's your next lesson. It's what to do in an emergency. Did you hear me now that you've got the blasted ear buds out."

"Dad, stay calm. I don't know why you're so upset. You keep telling me that I never listen to you anyway, so what difference does it make if my earbuds are in or out?"

"I'm calling a tow. We can't drive the car now."

When the AAA truck stopped just in front of the car, the driver futilely tried to stifle a laugh before he went to work.

Walter dreaded the requisite call home. "Are you all right?" Jane queried.

Now, on this second venture, the memories of that first disaster haunted Walter's mind. On that first sally, at least no one was hurt. He feared the worst was to come.

"Dad, you're like weirded out," Paige chipped in.

He was. He handed over his car keys to Paige, who snatched them eagerly. Then Walter closed his eyes and at a funereal pace walked out of the house, over to the car, and slid into the front seat, passenger side.

"Don't forget the dog food,"

"I won't," he shot back.

Then, he quickly forgot all about the mission to get dog food. Walter's mind slipped back to the front lines of World War I. "Out of the trenches, men. We've got the Hun on the run. Those dirty bastards mined the field in front of us, but I've mapped out a safe path. We stick together. You hear, stick together. Veer to the right. Veer to the right. Do you hear me?" The stalwart platoon leader took out his whistle, blew it with all his might, jumped out of the trench, his .45 pistol blaring out death and destruction. "Veer to the right, men. Veer to the veer to the right." One of his men had broken from the group—a sudden jolt!

"Dad, what are you talking about?" Paige heard her father as her mother had instructed her to put her ear buds away.

Walter's eyes bulged out as if to burst. "Veer left, Paige. You're going over the curb and onto the walkway."

"Dad, you told me to drive on the right."

"But not that far," The rear bumper bounced as it scraped the curb. Paige had straightened the car out.

"Let's go home, Paige." Walter mumbled as his right hand turned a ghastly white clutching the door handle.

"But what about the dog food?"

"Don't worry about the dog food. When we get back, I'll take me a long pleasant walk and get the dog food."

When they returned, Paige stomped upstairs to her room. Jane stood tall, her arms akimbo. "Another pleasant outing? Well, at least you got the dog food." Walter just looked down at the floor. "So, no dog food, and now Paige is all upset."

"I'll walk to the store and get the dog food," Walter replied in hushed, chastened tones.

"Walter, if you're going to walk to the store, just remember that you promised to help Tommy with his algebra homework. Get the algebra done and then take your walk."

"I won't forget." Then Walter's mind turned to the famous mathematicians of old. "Euclid, Pythagoras, Newton, and then there was Katherine Johnson, who made calculations for orbital mechanics. I remember some newscaster on the television saying that." Walter delved deeply in thought even if he had utterly no clue what orbital mechanics was, is, or shall be. "But algebra, there's the rub. I recall something about an Arabian philosopher and mathematician. Muhammad Ibn Musa al-Khan—something or other. I can't really get a fix on the totality of his name." Walter's mind drifted to a palace library in the ninth century, where a turbaned, bearded great figure stroked his beard with one hand and with the other solved the mysteries of solving for X. "X marks the spot, so they say. But that was for eighteen century pirates, not for the ninth century mathematical genius Muhammad. He had access to the palace library. I wonder what else he had access to?" Walter's mind drifted over to nubile, bare- stomached dancing girls, who resembled Disney-like cartoon characters. "But Muhammad Ibn Musa—whatever his name— fixated on the mysteries of X, not of adolescent cravings for gyrating dancing girls. He was a genius while I am—"

"Dad, you've got to help me with this word problem."

Few phrases stoked the fiery flames of volcanic eruptions from the gut of dormant fears more than the seemingly simple expression—"word problem."

"Tommy, what is it? I mean the word problem."

"It's something about some dork named Xavier. I mean, who names their kid *Xavier*?"

Walter cringed a bit, recalling the shame he felt about his own name. "As much as I want to be called *Tony,* no one calls me that," Walter reflected. Finally, gathering whatever paternal pride he still had left after the Paige incident, Walter asked, "So what is the word problem, Tommy?"

"Well, it goes like this, Pops." Walter hated being called *Pops* even more than he loathed being called *Walter,* but he gritted his teeth and thought of getting revenge on his own little Tommy. "OK, Pops, it goes like this: 'Xavier will be three times his present age in four years. What is Xavier's present age?' I mean in addition to having a dorky name, who really cares about how old the dork is?"

Walter reached down into memories decades past of solving algebra problems and also plunged the depths of his own lust for revenge at being called *Pops.* "Well, Tommy-Boy, it goes like this." Walter paused to check his son's reaction to being called *Tommy-Boy.* Walter had achieved the desired effect. But, in a fleeting moment of early adolescent maturity, his son suppressed the anger he was feeling. All he wanted to do was to get his homework done. Then he would be free for whatever was left of the night.

Sensing his own immaturity at seeking revenge, Walter composed his face into that of a pedantic pedagogue and stated, "The issue here is solving for *X.* But first we must translate the words into a mathematical expression, an equation if you will."

"OK, Dad, that's all well and good, but what's the answer?"

"The answer is not as important as the journey of discovery," Walter pontificated.

"Yeah, yeah, yeah, you sound like my teacher. So, what's the translation?"

"$3X = X + 4$, the 4 referring to the 4 year time period. *X,* of course, refers to the unknown, Xavier's current age."

"So, how old is this Xavier dude?"

"We must review the process of solving for *X.* We want to simplify terms so that the equation states simply, X equals the answer." Walter wondered how in the afterlife Muhammad Ibn Must—whatever his name would regard his explanation. Walter had no beard to stroke, so he rubbed his chin.

"So, if I subtract an *X* from both sides of the equationI, we get 2X = 4.

If I then divide both sides by 2, I get X = 2." Walter took a fleeting pride in his explanation.

"That dork Xavier is 2. I knew that all along, 'cause if the dude were any older, he'd probably change his tag to like 'Call me X.'" Then Tommy raced upstairs to finish the rest of his math homework and finally find that freedom he so yearned for.

Walter continued rubbing his chin.

"Walter, what's wrong with your chin? Have you got a rash or something?" Jane asked him matter-of-factly. "Since you are on your way to the store to get dog food, you might as well pick up a few more things. I've made a list for you."

Walter scanned the list. "There must be twenty or more items here. I can't carry all that back with me."

"Sorry to spoil your walk. You'll have to drive there."

Water turned a ghastly white. "Don't worry, Dear. Paige is on the phone with one of her girl friends. She'll probably still be on the phone when you come back."

"All right," Water whispered in response. He glanced upstairs and then to the right and then to the left. All clear. He took slow, deliberate steps, still clutching the grocery list in his left hand. He reserved his right hand for any emergency that might arise. Once again, entangled in a web of illusion and dreams, he made his way to the car, stopping briefly to review his commission. "You, Sir Walter, have been commissioned a most dangerous and secretive and essential quest by Her Majesty, Queen Jane. You are to speak to no one except, if necessary to allay any suspicions. Miscreants and scoundrels abound at every turn. Accomplish what the Queen has detailed in your commands and see to it that none—no one, I say—learns of the exact purpose of your commissioned quest."

"I will, your Majesty, do as you request." Then the newly commissioned Sir Walter plopped himself on his trusty steed, a slightly rusted but still functioning 1999 Ford with 199,000 miles on it. "Onward, mighty war-horse, onward. Duty never waits." Walter turned the ignition key. With a billow of smoke, his valiant vehicle chugged at first, then took off in a frenzy of screeching tires.

"What the hell is Walter doing now?" wondered Jane. Even Paige paused her philippic against the history teacher who had asked her for her homework (an assignment she hadn't done)."Just who does he think he is anyway? I mean I'll do it eventually, I guess."

Tearing out of the driveway onto the public domain, Sir Walter heard screaming sirens and suspected flashing red lights. "Dragons, no doubt," he spoke out loud to no one but himself. But, as he turned onto Enchanted Parkway, he felt his throat tighten as he suspected the worst. He continuously glanced to the left and to the right and kept an eagle eye on his rearview mirror. "The red eyed beast comes from behind you to catch you unaware," he kept reminding himself. But, there were no red eyed dragons out that night. He reached his destination. "Half the quest is done," Sir Walter consoled himself with the thought. Onward, onward, strode he to the glass sliding doors of the SuperSaver supermarket.

"Hey, buddy, you there, you got a little spare change to help out an old, homeless guy?"

Sir Walter halted. He had a duty to perform, but he also had a conscience to uphold. "Wasn't charity towards the poor and helpless part and parcel of the chivalric code he had sworn to uphold?" He took out his wallet, peered int it, took out a bill, and handed it over to the destitute beggar.

"Hey, you gotta have more than this. I mean, what the hell do you expect me to buy with a measly dollar, you cheap bastard!"

Sir Walter repressed his instinct the slay the miscreant for the assault on his honor, but he restrained his primal instinct for revenge and hurried on to complete his quest.

The journey home found the valiant knight looking left, looking right, looking in his rearview mirror—everywhere but right in front of him. Awakened from his reverie by the fearsome glare of tail lights, Walter slammed on the brakes, narrowly missing the car in front of him. "Hey, buddy, watch where you're goin'" shouted the driver in front of him—a driver who bore an uncanny resemblance to the beggar who had accosted him earlier. Walter shook his head. "It can't be the same fellow. This fellow—the one I almost smashed—was driving a late model Lexus. But, I can't forget that voice and the jarring, snide 'Hey, buddy,' voice. Unless, of course, it must be witchcraft, wizardly work of one who had sealed his fate with a compact with the devil. Yes, that's it. Oh, how could I have been such a fool."

At last, Walter returned to his driveway, bearing the two bags of groceries. "Walter, did you get everything on the list? Let's see." Jane—aka Lady Jane, Queen Jane—emptied each bag and noted the contents: "bread, eggs, butter, bacon—Walter, you know we always buy turkey bacon and here you bought pork bacon—frozen peas, blueberries, plain yogurt, green beans, broccoli, tomatoes, a ten pound bag of potatoes—Walter, I told you to buy only a five pound bag—cucumber, radishes, carrots, lettuce, sweet peppers, Lucky Charms cereal, salami, and a three pound roll of hamburger. Walter, I count nineteen items, not twenty. What did you forget?"

"Dog food?" He replied sheepishly.

"Walter, you're hopeless, but I love you. At least you don't drink or do drugs—or do you?"

Walter had already accepted his fate, turned towards the living room where his recliner awaited him. He turned on the TV, seeing a tuxedo clad Marlon Brando softly giving commands in a dusty voice to friends and foes alike. Walter would be no more. He would be Tony, a Mafioso don and godfather.

"But doesn't the godfather get shot? No, on second thought, I'll turn my hand to writing short stories in my own fictional world."

"Walter, for crying out loud, pick up the dog food tomorrow on your way home from work."

"Of course, Dear, of course."

51

"You'd think that by now he would have had it."

"Maybe he could just graciously step aside and give the rest of us a chance."

"There's no way he would do that. He's too old and too obsessive to do that."

"Maybe he could start thinking about the rest of us. He's had his turn. Now it's time for him to move on."

"Yeah, I could use a shot at his job."

"He's just a bitter old workaholic. He's hanging on just to spite the rest of us."

"He could use a life. Maybe we could help him get one."

The lunch room banter quickly turned to silence as Dan Reilly pushed the door open and stood there, fixing his gaze on the seven middle aged workers—he wouldn't call them colleagues—who wanted him out of their way. Dan knew what they had been talking about in his absence. They always harped on the same discordant tune" "So, Dan, when are you going to retire?" The cabal of seven had already pleaded their case before upper management who had heeded their call. Dan was demoted—the hope being that this affront would goad him into retirement. It didn't. Dan just kept on working and saying nothing. He knew that the next stage would be to fire him. He could threaten an age discrimination suit, but such a move would just postpone the inevitable. Besides, Dan had something far better in mind.

The oldest of the lunchroom seven, a woman with the ambition of making upper management before she turned forty, stood there stolidly, arms akimbo, and challenged Dan. "So, just when, Mr. Reilly, may we plan the retirement party?"

"Oh, for whom? I didn't realize anyone was retiring."

11

"Dan, you know what I mean."

"Oh, do you refer to me?"

The other six were glaring at Dan, who projected just a barely visible smirk. He seemed to be enjoying the whole scene. Then he announced, "Well, you won't have to wait long. I just need to reach fifty-one. Then you can have your party."

"Dan, you haven't been fifty- one in over a decade. Are you going senile on us? If so, then that's all the more reason to get out while you still have some thin shred of sanity left." Martha never minced words—at least not to anyone she considered a subordinate. Clearly she felt Dan belonged to that lowly classification. Martha wore her hair straight down, cut Cleopatra style. She worked long hours, generally staying past ten pm, her large cubicle piled high with stacks of papers. Some of her fellow lunchroom cabal started rumors that she stayed late so that she could carry on a sordid lusty affair with the night custodian, a good natured but toothless fellow who probably feared Martha rather than lusted after her. So that gossip never went anywhere. Actually none of the employees who knew Martha would even nibble at this sordid fare. It did provide a fleeting moment of titillation for the bored and distracted employees. Besides, everyone knew that, if Martha were to have an affair, it would be only with someone who could advance her career. Her single-minded ambition prompted her colleagues to both fear, adore, loathe and love her.

Once Martha realized that Dan didn't respond to her insult in the way she had hoped, she convinced herself that Dan really was going senile. She threw up her hands in disgust when Dan almost chuckled. "Just fifty-one and I'm almost there, just fifty-one."

"Dan, can't you exit with a just a shred of decency?

Just then B. T. Intervened or at least try to play the role of mediator. In reality, he was just as ambitious as Martha, but his approach to getting ahead was to play the good-ole-boy.

He raised his hand to signal his intervention. "Dan, Martha's just looking out for you. I mean you've worked here for forty years. That's long enough for anyone. You deserve a rest and an opportunity to do all of those things you've dreamed of doing. You know, go fishing, hell, sleep in on a weekday, take a trip or two. Do you play golf? Go to the range. Hit some balls. Have some fun. Just do anything other than to hang around here."

B. T. beamed as he delivered these lines, envisioning himself as a wise and benevolent pastor or, even better, as a TV psychologist, dispensing advice and consoling the weary, the weak, and the senile. Even though he was Dan's junior by several decades, he smiled benevolently and assumed a patriarchal air of wisdom.

Dan smiled back, rubbed his chin a bit, and replied, "The answer is still 51." Then he turned aside and briskly strode away.

"That, my friends, is one weird puppy," B.T. pronounced with all the gravity he could muster.

"He's worse than that, B. T. He's dangerous. Who knows what he's plotting with all that fifty-one nonsense. I'm going to see Larry and put an end to this ludicrous little game that old dotard is playing." Martha stormed upstairs to the lofty domain of upper management just as she had months earlier when she had succeeded in getting Dan demoted. She'd fuss and fume, accuse Dan of of breaking up the close-knit family of colleagues and she might just get her way. In any event, she could always win more begging rights to have dwelt, if only for a moment, in the upper stratosphere of the company.

From past experience, Dan had correctly guessed what Martha would do and prepared for the phone call that would state with the succinct and direct message: "Come to Larry's office immediately." He complied and headed up the stairs. Martha's eyes followed as he slowly made his way to his fate or so surmised Martha.

B. T., however, was astounded. "Did you spot that goofy fatuous grin? He's worse off than I thought. Doesn't he know he's headed to his execution?" B. T. Carefully redesigned his posture and facial expression. He held his left hand on his forehead; with his right hand he made a fist. His lips parted into almost a snarl. "Maybe you're right, Martha. Maybe he is dangerous. Do you think Larry is safe?"

Martha responded decisively. "I'm calling Security right now. We've got to head off this coming disaster. Who knows what Dangerous Dan will do?"

When Dan checked in with Larry's secretary, he still maintained that same silly smile. He was smiling still when he decorously knocked three times on Larry's door. Then he opened it when a gruff voice pronounced, "Come in." Larry was poring over some spreadsheets. After a few minutes, he looked up at Dan, who still sported that smile and stood there stoically as Larry finished whatever it was that he was reading.

"Sit down, Dan. We need to talk." Then, Larry paused as if weighing every word carefully. "You've been with us a long time, Dan."

Dan complied, sat down, and matter-of-factly responded, "Yes, I have."

Larry rubbed his brow as if he were trying to put in just the right words. He leaned back in his chair, pursed his lips and finally let out an emphatic "But—"

"Well, Larry, you were going to say something like 'Some say, perhaps, too long.'"

"Ah, well, yes, Dan, something like that."

"Have you read the latest performance reviews?"

"No, Dan, I haven't gotten around to that. I've just been too busy with this China deal."

"Well, Larry, that's not a problem. I brought along a complete copy as well as the executive summary. It seems that HR gave me the highest marks in the division in three categories: meeting all deadlines, establishing the best rapport with clients, having the best absentee record. In fact, in the last decade I've had the best absentee record in the company and the highest ratings."

"Well, Dan, that may all be true. But the are other factors, the intangibles, the camaraderie among colleagues, that team building, that esprit de corps."

"Oh, yes, Larry, you're quite right. Unfortunately some employees direct all or most of their efforts trying to build themselves up by tearing others down. Such behavior is reprehensible and violates that very family spirit you endeavor to maintain. It's such a tragedy that such intelligent employees waste so much time on negative behavior, a negativity that corrupts the entire enterprise, wouldn't you say? You've got a tough job, Larry, trying to deal with these malcontents."

Larry just sat there, stunned. He hadn't prepared for this type of reaction. Dan didn't sound dangerous, he didn't talk like some deranged lunatic, and—worst of all—he had embarrassed Larry by referring to performance reviews that he hadn't bothered to read.

Dan realized and relished in achieving the desired effect. If Larry wouldn't talk, he would. "Well, Larry, if you need to talk or even just vent, be assured that I'm ready and willing to listen. Don't hesitate to contact me. I am at your side ever willing to listen and, if necessary, act."

"Ah, yes, Dan, I'll do that."

"Well, Larry, thanks for our little chat. I do have to finish that earnings report. Can't be late you know. The stockholders wouldn't stomach it."

Dan did a quick about face, strolled out of the room, smiled at the secretary, who, he knew, couldn't stand Martha and B.T. Then he whispered under his breath, "Just fifty-one. That's all I'll need."

But, before Dan entered the lair of his co-workers, he paused, allowing himself time to compose his features. His gait stiffened and slowed, his face was cast downward, his fingers clasped his shirtsleeves. He would transform himself into the dismissed and guilty castoff, walking the plank into the frigid waters of unemployment. He pushed the door open only a few inches, the feeble effort of one consumed with misery over his presumed fate. Then, with two more infirm exertions, he managed to push the door open just enough that he could angle his way in. Once within eyeshot of his colleagues, he slackened his pace even more, lowered his gaze even further as if staring into the abyss of despair, his right hand supporting his forehead. Such melodramatic gestures were not in vain. He had achieved the desired effect. Co-workers gazed and, perhaps even sympathized, maintaining a frozen silence. B. T. thought momentarily of offering a few words of condolence but checked himself, not willing to break the somber mood. Only Martha let slip a thin sneer of triumph. Dan retreated to his desk, made a show of packing a few personal items, and then announced that he was leaving early. No one said a word.

Dan stopped by the Men's Room in the lobby before he left. There, while washing his hands, he looked at himself in the mirror. His hair was thinning, even balding. Soon, he could dispense with a hair cut, for nothing was left to cut. He stared glumly at the bags under his eyes. Then he surprised himself. He took off his shirt and looked at himself in the mirror. He wasn't twenty-nine any more. He had a small paunch, but the muscles in his forearm still rippled and he still had defined biceps. "What a fool I am! I'm not some high school sophomore, trying to convince himself of some budding masculinity. I work with my brain far more than my brawn—or what's left of my brawn." He put his shirt back on. As he buttoned his shirt, another man entered the restroom and glanced over at him and shrugged his shoulders as if saying, "What the hell, to each his own." Then he washed his hands and left. "I guess I'm just a little too pre-occupied with myself. Well, back to business."

Once out of the office, Dan's stride assumed a renewed vigor. He didn't have just a spring in his step. He had a resounding bounce. His vehicle was easy to spot on the lot reserved for employees. Among all the sporty SUV's, his slightly battered Ford F-150 truck with 189,000+ miles on it as well as a few rust spots stood out. "Old, but still chugging along—my second self." He'd go home, fix dinner for himself and his wife Sue. She worked three twelve hour shifts a week—at least the shifts were supposed to last twelve hours. Most of the time, the twelve hours extended to thirteen or fourteen hours, and occasionally more. "I'll fire up the grill and barbecue some hamburgers along with some peppers and corn and a salad. She'll like that, and so will I. We've finally got the fifty-one. I can feel it."

But, when he pulled in the driveway, he noticed that Sue's car was already there. "What's up?" He wondered. Then, as he pulled in the door, he saw the table already set. There was even a wine glass out and a decanter they hadn't used in decades. It was a wedding gift that they used only on special occasions. Sue rushed down the stairs and flung her arms around Dan. "We've done it, Dan. In fact, we've even more than done it."

"You mean we've reached fifty-one?"

Sue kissed him on the cheek and responded with feigned sorrow: "No, Dan, not fifty-one." Then she paused for effect before bursting out, "Fifty-four. We've done it, Dan. In fact we've more than done it. The broker called and left a message for me at work. I guess you had already stepped out. Anyway, we now own fifty-four percent of the stock. Even if every other investor would oppose us, we'd still have a clear majority. We own the company, Dan. We've done it."

Dan simply said, "Of course. I knew we'd do it. And now we have." He kissed his wife and then sat down to a regal feast in the middle of the week.

But the next day at work, Dan couldn't restrain himself. He had to maintain the charade. Alone and forlorn, he pulled into his parking space. Alone and forlorn, he trudged wearily from the parking lot to his small desk. Alone and forlorn, he wearily lowered his body onto his chair. Alone and forlorn, he opened his desk, took out a few personal items and then shut it definitively. He the rested his forehead on his two hands.

His colleagues looked on, some sympathetically reflecting. "Well, the old dinosaur is gone. RIP, Dan." Others, especially Martha, relished the moment. "We've done it, we've done it. That decrepit old fool is gone at last. I'm so glad I went to see Larry yesterday."

As if on cue, Larry did come down from above, escorting Mrs. Susan Reilly, who appeared resplendent in a glimmering gold formal dress accented by an ebony scarf. Dan took a few items from his desk, pocketed them and then stood up. Larry, extended his hand. Dan shook his hand and then the threesome stood before all of Dan's former co-workers. "Ladies and gentlemen, please applaud the new majority stockholders." Instead of applause, there was a stunned silence. Dan and Sue grinned and took the elevator upstairs to the boardroom. Larry stayed downstairs.

Martha and B. T. Both burst out. "It couldn't be. It wasn't supposed to end this way."

"But it did. You two and everyone else have a lot to learn."

"You mean when Dan was fatuously mumbling some idiocy about fifty-one, he was all the while intent on owning fifty-one percent of the company's stock?" Martha couldn't contain her shock and awe.

"Well, Sue and Dan don't own fifty-one percent of the stock." Here, wanting to continue the game, Larry paused and assessed the stunned, dumbstruck workers. "The couple owns fifty-four per cent of the stock. They're the majority owners and, in effect, own the company. Dan will be spending most of his time in the board room." Martha and B. T. turned a ghastly white. "Oh, don't worry. He won't be meddling in personnel matters. He's got bigger fish to fry. I'll admit that I was as stunned as everyone else when I heard the news. Dan and Sue have been investing in our company for over three decades. When the stock slipped a bit, the couple took advantage of the situation and bought as many shares as they could. They lived simply, scrimped and saved until they could make another purchase when the price was right. Every year, they added just a little more to their holdings. Now they're the majority holders. I heard that Dan has also been studying new ways—including Artificial Intelligence— to make the company even more profitable. The two will be a real asset."

"But, how?" Martha objected. "It wasn't supposed to be this way."

"But it is," Larry concluded. "We've all got a lot to learn from Dan and Sue."

SAN JUDASCO

(In Recognition of St. Jude, the Patron Saint of Lost Causes)

At eleven in the morning, give or take a few minutes—everything was give or take a few in Thad's world—Thaddeus Weisz coughed and groaned his way into a bleary consciousness. His oversized toes began scratching the sand, as he eased himself into contact with the rest of the world. He straightened out his sand-encrusted toes. Hs knees creaked a bit as they, too, returned to active duty. Then his hips arched and his arms stretched out to the late morning sun. Through half-opened eyes, he mustered a few words filtered through a voice made guttural by a heavy mix of tobacco and pot smoke. He belted out to no one in particular, "What the hell time is it?" Through bloodshot eyes, he spied the clock. "Aw, hell, it's eleven." He was supposed to meet his childhood friend Tom Young and his family for a snorkeling trip. He slipped on worn, faded jeans, tattered in a a few places with white threads showing through and leather sandals. Then he took a quick glance at the mirror and smoothed out his hair graying at the temples. "Not bad for a guy pushing fifty," he declared definitively. His suntanned belly wasn't flabby, but over the years it had lost some of its definition as his prized six-pack had eased out to one single flat surface. He took a few strides over to the bar, as his bedroom lay just off to the right for convenience, and grabbed a quick cup of coffee.

Then he went marching off, seeking Tom Young, his wife, and their two children. He strode over to the snorkel shack and got the answer he was hoping for. "Yes, Mr. Young and his family had rented some snorkeling equipment and went out with a guide around ten-twenty. He said something about waiting for you, but I told him not to wait or worry. Just go. Thad won't care." He didn't. Besides, as owner of Mañana Mama's bar, he had to plan carefully for two events: his gala New Year's Eve party and an individual rendezvous with a to-be-determined young lady.

He had devoted weeks to preparing for this party as his business nose-dived in January and early February before picking up again with the rowdy spring breakers pouring booze into their guts and money into his bank account. He paid his full-time barkeeper well—well enough by local standards, that is—and had hired the barkeeper's cousin for the anticipated surge at New Year's Eve bash. Fernando, Thad's full-time man, would take care of all the mixed drink orders and Tomas, his cousin, would handle all the beer and wine orders. Marta, Fernando's wife, had been preparing appetizers: churros, fish tacos, quesadillas, a little guacamole, sopes, but above all else, lots of salty chips with lots of salty dips. Thad had recalled the advice the former owner of the bar had given him some twenty years ago when he had decided to become an expatriate American and live his life in the shadow of palm trees and sun drenched sand. "The more salt they eat, the more thy drink, and the more they drink the more money I make." Thad had taken this advice to heart and made a decent living by it. He had spent the last few days handing out a free drink card to anyone and everyone he saw. Thad figured that, if that first drink was good enough and strong enough, they would stay. He had arranged with Fernando to make that first drink strong—he could water down subsequent drinks. Normally, customers shimmied their way up to the bar and ordered their own drinks, but not tonight. Fernando's and Marta's two teenage daughters would act as waitresses as they had for the last two years, making more in tips on that one night than they would make in a month at their full-time jobs. The two sisters would hand-stitch and embroider blouses and shirts that they sold in a makeshift store just off the main highway. When Thad returned to the bar, Marta was already cooking in the small kitchen, and Fernando was taking stock of the liquor supply. "Enough tequila, but not enough beer, boss. Last year we almost ran out. We've got enough Corona for the tourists, but most of the locals like Tecate or Sol. Should I pick up six more cases of each?"

"You're my man, Fernando. If we don't run out tonight, we ought to be able to sell off the remainder in the six weeks before spring break." Thad looked around and thought to himself, "Things are looking good here. Now for the next task."

He couldn't prepare for the next task, but had to await, and Fate had generally obliged him. However, in the last three years, Thad had had a little more trouble than he had had in the past. He was looking for a girl, a quick one-night-stand with the "swimming-with-the-dolphins" type. After all, it would be New Year's Eve, and for the last twenty years he had rung in the new year with some twenty something (or sometimes a bit younger). The two of them had always exchanged telephone numbers or, more lately email addresses; however, once that earnest promise to keep in contact had been sealed with a kiss, he had never heard a word from his partner of the evening. He hadn't bothered to keep in contact and neither had she. Somehow the whole exchange of contact thing had rendered the whole matter less seedy. In earlier years, Thad had made his connection early sometimes as early as a week in advance. He would have taken his chosen mate snorkeling or scuba diving before bedding her down on the holiday eve. But, in these last three years, he had had to wait until New Year's Eve to stalk and overtake his prey. "All in good time," he had assured himself.

Then his prayers were answered. At noon, into the bar sauntered a long-legged, blonde haired, twenty something (maybe a bit younger) woman looking for a youth hostel. She wore her hair in a ponytail that extended from the back of her U-Cal baseball cap. She had tied up her worn t-shirt so that her midriff was exposed, and her tattered, threadbare jeans had been cut off mid thigh. She swung her backpack down to the floor, looking tired but oddly spirited at the same time.

"Fernando, a drink for the young lady, on the house, of course." As Thad said this, Fernando obliged, to what had become his boss's routine year after year. He winked at Thad and made sure that the drink was strong and sweet. "So, what brings you to San Judasco? It's a little off the beaten path." Through long practice, Thad could sound almost disinterested, merely inquisitive.

"Oh, I'm always looking to be off that same old beaten path. I like to tempt the new. I hear there's good snorkeling here."

"The best. You can see turtles, rays, barracudas, even a few dolphins. I can show you if you like."

She paused and took a few sips from the drink that Fernando had left her. She flipped off her cap, took a few more sips, and then replied. "Yeah, that would be great. Let me finish my drink." She downed the rest of the drink in one long draught with a flourish and a bit of bravado.

"Fernando, another drink for my friend." Thad quickly ordered with a wave of his hand. This time she didn't bother sipping.

By the time she had downed a third and a fourth drink, all thoughts of swimming with the dolphins or turtles, or with anything else for that matter had disappeared from her head. Thad took her over to his bedroom and left her there to sleep off her hangover. He knew that to win her affection, even for just one night, he had to play the role of her guardian angel. So, he laid her gently down, taking care not to rouse her. He even changed the dust and sweat stained pillowcase for a new, fresh one, having long forgotten when he had done that last. He covered her with a light blanket. Thad realized that she was no experienced drinker, who would have measured out her drinks, allowing each one to settle in before taking another. Thad then gazed at her trim, slender—almost anorexic— form. "I wonder when was the last time she had had anything to eat?" Thad questioned himself. As he turned out of his room, he paused, took one long look at the sleeping form and said to himself, "God, she's young. Hell, she could even be my daughter for all I know."

Fernando said nothing but busied himself with slicing limes and making the bar ready for the onslaught that would come in a few hours. In his mind, he, too, wondered how long Thad could keep pretending he was twenty years or more younger. But, he had to keep his thoughts to himself, as his boss paid well, and gave his family opportunities that otherwise they would not have had. Marta remained oblivious to it all, occupying herself with cooking and with her display of red underwear, which she sold for good luck on the New Year.

Thad sat quietly by the bar for half an hour or so before his friend Tom, his wife Cynthia, and their two children, Dan and Tom Junior, broke the silence."Hey, Thad we wanted to wait for you, but the guy at the snorkel shack told us not to, something about getting ready for the New Year—then noticing the half drawn curtain with an unfamiliar backpack lying on the floor, Tom said, "Yeah, I can see you've been busy" with almost a hint of envy that Cynthia couldn't ignore.

Luckily for Thad, the two boys couldn't contain themselves, so he was spared trying to explain backpacks and other details. Tom Junior almost spoke in superlatives. "It was just so awesome! I saw three or four turtles, big ones, must have weighed hundreds of pounds, and rays and one barracuda"

His brother wasn't quite so impressed. "That wasn't a barracuda, moron. That was just some old log floating under some guy's boat."

"Yeah, well, that log took off mighty quick. You're just mad you didn't see it."

"Yeah, well, I saw some stuff you didn't, giant ass goat fish or whatever they're called, bigger than anything I've ever seen."

"Yeah, Thad, it was just so awesome. We're going out tomorrow again. I can't wait to get back home and tell the guys."

"Thanks, Thad, the boys had a great time. " Cynthia added. "We knew you'd be busy with all the New Year's Eve preparations."

Thad couldn't tell whether she was being a bit facetious or not. She, too, had clearly seen the half-drawn curtain and probably had spied the sleeping form that had by now started snoring.. Thad had arranged for them to get free snorkeling and a cut rate at a nearby hotel. He had picked them up at the airport some sixty kilometers away, but he had also most definitely missed that ten o'clock appointment. He wan't sure, but he didn't think Cynthia thought very much of him. Still, she was Tom's wife, and he and Tom had gone a long way back before that twenty year long hiatus.

"Fernando, tres cervezas, por favor." Thad spoke Spanish to Fernando only when customers were present. Sometimes it was advantageous for Fernando to pretend he spoke only Spanish. The sprinkling in of a few Spanish phrases here and there also gave the bar, which pretty much resembled any other beach bar, a more exotic aura. Marta brought over some of her speciality dishes— freshly grilled fish tacos sprinkled with her home made pico de Gallo. She added some ceviche on the side. She then returned to the barbacao she was slow cooking in a hole dug into the sand following an ancient Mayan recipe. "She's the best cook around," Thad boasted. "She keeps customers coming back."

"Well, Thad, you've got that right, at least." Cynthia exclaimed after she had just taken a bite of a fish taco. Without even being asked, Marta had given the two boys two hamburgers each, which they had wolfed down as only adolescent boys could do. Tom had downed a beer even before he had taken a bite so Thad motioned for another one for his old friend. He knew the family would soon be ready for a siesta as the sun and the wind and the salt water had lulled them into a sleepy but satisfied mood.

"Thanks for everything, Thad. You've been a most generous host." Cynthia said this as a cue that the four of them would be leaving for a nap so that they could take in the end of the year festivities later that evening. Actually, Cynthia didn't know what to think of her husband's old friend. He could be incredibly generous and yet so self-centered at the same time. Likewise, Thad didn't know what to think of Cynthia. In twenty years, she had aged, but so had Tom, who now sported a small paunch. Yet, Tom seemed so happy. He could come home to Cynthia every night. Maybe they'd even make love when they weren't drunk. Over the years, Thad had had enjoyed many women, most of them drunk, as was he, so he wondered what it would be like to make love to the same woman for so long, stone-cold sober. Glancing over to the curtain that separated the bar from his bedroom, he caught sight of the sleeping form that had just turned over. "Well, that's all fine and good for Tom." He drained his last bottle of cold beer. What's-her-name was still sleeping—and snoring only now a little louder. Tom got up and gently rolled her over onto her side so she'd quiet down. In another hour or so, he'd wake her up.

With unexpected urgency, Thad sprang into action. He roamed the beach, handing out his one free drink coupon to everyone he encountered and boasted that he had the best bar on the beach for New Year's Eve or for any other day for that matter. The day before he had stationed some of the locals who spoke English in strategic spots along the beach. He had paid them to sing his praises. "Oh, yes, señor and señorita, Thad's place is the best there is. Everyone around here knows he's muy bueno."

By three o'clock, it was evident that Thad's plan was working. As an early crowd began filtering in to cash in their free drink and to pay for plenty more. Marta's food contributed to the staying power as did Fernando's two pretty daughters, who hustled drinks with a flair. It would be a great evening, Thad thought. He needed only one more ingredient to make the evening perfect. That one ingredient was slowly regaining consciousness.

When Thad checked in, he demurely knocked softly on the wooden door frame.The sleeping form slowly opened her eyes. "Oh, I'm so embarrassed."

"How about dinner tonight? Rumor has it that I've got the best cook in the Yucatan, and, at sunset, the beachfront view can't be beat. I'm Thad, the owner of this humble but proud establishment."

"Hi, I'm Constance. I'm so sorry. I—"

"Don't worry about it, Constance," Thad added as he gave her a gentle hug that was intended to be far more reassuring than it was erotic. "How about a little something to eat?"

"That would be great!" She replied far more eagerly than she had intended.

Thad asked Marta to bring over some cheese quesadillas and three fresh fish tacos. This Marta did with an exaggerated deference, bowing deeply and placing each plate down without a sound. Thad knew she was mocking him and figured that he deserved whatever mockery came his way. Still, he realized there was no way he could find another Marta. Perhaps, in the same way Tom knew he could never find another Cynthia—even if Tom did almost all of the cooking and probably a disproportionate amount of the eating.

Constance gobbled her food with the same gusto that Tom's two boys had shown earlier. Thad had been right. She hadn't eaten for a day, maybe more than a day. That's why she had passed out so quickly. When she had finished, she eyed Thad with a dreamy indulgence as if he had just rescued her from some fire dragon.

"Do you need a beer to wash that down with?" Thad was playing his benevolent, paternalistic role.

"Yeah, sure, that would be great."

"Dos cervezas, por favor, Fernando." Fernando didn't quite shrug off the request, but he did motion his cousin to perform his beer duties. Then he resumed his bartender duties, mixing margarita after margarita and strawberry daiquiri after strawberry daiquiri interspersed with a a few Tom Collins and whisky sodas. "Yes, it would be a fun night," Thad mused. "And the fun had just begun."

Constance stuck close to Thad's side the entire night as he greeted each customer. She, too, was playing a role. A casual observer might assume that she was a co-owner of Thad's beachside bar. Thad shook hands or hugged each guest. From long experience, he knew which customers he could hug and which ones he should not. He enthusiastically accepted each new free drink coupon as if he were the Santa Claus of barkeepers. Constance left his side only once to freshen up as she had claimed. She came back radiant and eased herself into the role of a gracious hostess. She had slipped into a pair of skin-tight black pants and a silky white blouse with a plunging neckline. "She must come from money even if she doesn't have any right now," Thad reflected. Her only flaw was that she had to keep pace with everyone's drinking. Thad. himself prudently strolled around the bar, sipping only a tonic water with a lime twist so that he could appear to be drinking even though he was not. "New Year's Eve was amateur night," he thought to himself. Just before sunset around six, he took everyone out to salute the falling sun, drink in hand. When he returned, he checked with Fernando and then put the initial receipts carefully away in a safe he had hidden below his bedroom. Excusing himself from Constance for the moment, he left her with a drink. "Yes, tonight would be a very good night, indeed. Fernando had been right about ordering extra beer. Above all else, we can't run out."

At six-thirty, Tom and his family arrived, dressed a little too formally for a beach bar but welcome nonetheless. Tom looked happy in his coat and tie, beaming contentedly with a smile stretching across his face. And Cynthia looked far better in a dress than she did in a swimsuit. Even Thad was impressed. But he had more guests to welcome and, with Constance draping her arm around him for support, had to walk for two. More and more people had crowded into the bar, making it seem that this was, without a doubt, the best bar on the beach as Thad and his paid promoters had boasted. At nine o'clock, Marta served her famous barbacao, succulent hunks of meat slow cooked for hours, wrapped in nopales. The locals knew that this delight was coming and arrived in droves shortly ahead of the serving. People ate and drank and toasted the New Year prematurely. Some would most definitely not make it until midnight. That's why, Thad knew, he could not postpone the entree past nine o'clock. By ten-thirty, Tom and Cynthia excused themselves. "We've got to check on the boys," Tom said and he meant it. Then he added, "To tell the truth, we've had such a great time that I don't know how to thank you, Thad. You've got the life."

"No thanks needed, Tom, anything for an old friend."

"Thad, you must be the most generous man in the world," Constance blurted out.

"No, no, I'm not." Thad shook Tom's hand and gently hugged Cynthia. Then the couple made their way back to their hotel. "I was playing the role of the generous host." Thad blurted out.

"You can't trick me, Thad. How about another drink?" She slurred her words a bit.

"Sure, I'll go get you one, but after that you'd better slow down." Thad checked himself and muttered, "God, I'm starting to sound more like her father than her seducer."

Shortly before midnight, Thad laid out an assortment of silly hats and cheap noisemakers. He had already arranged with Fernando to hand out some cheap champagne, imitation stuff. "By midnight, most of them will be so drunk that they couldn't tell the difference anyway," he had assured himself. So the new year was toasted and heralded in. By one-thirty all of customers had left. Even Marta and Fernando and their two daughters had taken their leave. There would be some cleaning to do tomorrow morning, but Thad had taken care of that to-do item by hiring a few of the local boys to take care of the mess. He could expect a late breakfast crowd, starting at nine o'clock and had tequila sunrises and bloody Marys ready. From a business angle, he had surpassed his expectations. He put away the receipts while Constance draped herself around a cup of strong coffee. Now he had to work on the personal level to make the night complete. After he had secured the night's receipts, he took out a stash of pot and rolled two joints, one for himself and one for Constance. From lengthy experience, he knew that he could secure himself a night of pleasure with just a little pot, a kind of dessert after the main course of alcohol. He took Constance out to a rocky small peninsula that jutted out into the bay. Here the couple took in long dreamy looks at the crescent moon overhead as they took a few drags. In a few minutes, Thad escorted Constance back to his bedroom.

"After I smoke pot, I just want to have sex," Constance muttered as she fumbled around taking off her blouse. She lay down on the bed and started to take off her pants but passed out after she had unbuttoned her waist. Thad completed the job she had started. But then, as he stood to pull down his pants, he just stared at her naked body, young and supple, just like like the ones he had seen for over twenty years. Oh, they might be different, the breasts might be bigger or smaller, the body a little different in complexion, but he concluded that he had been making love to the same being all these years, his version of monogamy. He pulled his pants up. Maybe it would be nice to grow old with somebody. Maybe Tom was right and he was wrong. Oh, Tom said that the envied him, but did he? Now Thad took his first drink of the night and stretched out next to Constance.

By seven-thirty, the sun shone brightly through the wooden slats in Thad's bedroom and he began stirring. The boys would be coming soon to clean and he had to be ready. He kissed Constance awake.

Once she had regained consciousness, she dreamily asked, "Well, how was I?"

"The best ever. I could hardly keep up with you." Thad smiled as he patted her thigh.

Constance dressed herself and asked for a pad of paper. "We can exchange emails, you now, keep in touch."

Thad knew the routine and also knew that the email address would be lost or forgotten. Still, he went along with the charade.

"Does the collectivo run to Tulum? I've heard that they've got the best youth hostels there."

"Yes, it does, and yes, the youth hostels there are great," Thad replied in a voice that had suddenly turned deadpan.

"I've got to run, Thad. You were great, too." Constance proclaimed as she kissed him on the cheek. The morning sun must have made him look older as it highlighted a few wrinkles around the eyes and a touch of grey at the temples.

"We'll keep in touch," Thad lied as he had lied so many times before, but this time he genuinely regretted the lie.

Just as Constance left, Fernando stepped in. "The usual, boss."

"Yeah, Fernando, the usual." Thad sipped a tequila sunrise slowly until a crowd of blood shot eyes and unsteady steps made their way in for a breakfast of huevos rancheros that Marta had been cooking. "Yeah, the usual," Thad repeated. Then he walked over to the snorkeling shack and waited until ten in case Tom and his family showed up, but they had made other plans.

JOURNEY: A ROADTRIP TO NOWHERE

"Hey, look at that: guts and gore just smashed into the concrete! Awesome!" Twelve year old Sam had glued his face to the car window and stared out at the material remains of a 'possum ground down into the unyielding concrete.

"Sam, you're grosser than that roadkill," Mindy, Sam's sister burst out, her eyes shooting out disgust and adolescent certainty.. "You're just like obsessed with the grossness of it all. In fact, you're just grossed out to the max." Mindy flatly determined.

I was intent on just driving on and letting it go. But Amanda assumed her maternal role and turned to stare down both of her children. "The two of you need to do something other than getting on each other's nerves. Why don't you read a book or even take in the sights—not the gross ones—or just sleep or something."

"Oh, Mom," brother and sister responded, one of the few times both could agree on anything.

I could have added to the discussion but decided not to. The two had dozed off to that half waking / half sleeping attitude of resignation. "What is it with the old people?" They must have been thinking.

The sighting of roadkill had become so common that it almost dulled the senses and the sensibilities. Still, it just didn't seem right to have the earthly remains of even an opossum just ground down into the pavement by cars and trucks speeding by. Not even a 'possum deserved that fate. Years ago, probably even decades ago, I had killed and eaten some 'possum. Perhaps that wasn't right but perhaps killing and devouring anything isn't right, but we routinely eat meat and that cycle means that someone, somewhere has to do the killing and butchering—not a pretty sight. Well, anyway the 'possum meat tasted a bit gamey, the flavorful stench of death and decay. So, I didn't eat 'possum after that adolescent indulgence. I just don't think there's much of a market for 'possum meat. But, anyway—

"Look out, John!" Yelled Amanda, who sat beside me on this leg of the trip. "Armadillo!" I did look out but not in time. The three-ton mass of the car raced to collide with the twelve pound victim. Before I could change lanes, the poor creature jumped up as armadillos do and embraced its grisly fate.

"Great job, Dad. You just smashed the guts out of that thing," Sam burst out.

"Why don't you grow up, Sam?" Mindy retorted. "Dad didn't want to kill that armadillo, right, Dad?"

This time, I couldn't evade the question. "No, I didn't. I don't like killing for the sake of killing."

"Yeah, but you can't deny how you you did a hell of a job, blasting away those armadillo guts all over the road, right, Dad?"

This time I didn't answer, preferring not to acknowledge the validity of my son's question. I didn't intend to kill but I had to wash off the blood and gore, just washing away any sign of carnage. But, who am I kidding. I'm no hero or villain, no Pontius Pilate nor grand inquisitor, just a middle-aged guy getting a little flabby, putting on some fat, sort of a human 'possum. I don't think I'd taste too good for any band of cannibals to feast on.

So, we pushed onward another couple of hundred miles. Then Amanda and I would change places, and she'd be driving the next leg of our trip while I would just doze off a bit and try to keep Mindy and Sam from dishing out verbal dings at each other.

We had planned this vacation on a whim. Amanda and Mindy had become intrigued with the idea of a road trip to the American Southwest, a harsh land of desert and scorching sun but also one of beauty. I had just wanted to take a road trip somewhere, someplace just to escape the stifling confines of my job and the monotony and grind of the daily routine. Sam was hoping to catch glimpses of Mustangs and cowboys, gunfights and blazing pistols. I had to let him know that, if he wanted to see gunfights, we had plenty of those at home. None were a pretty sight.

And, so we rode on. Soon I had relaxed a bit, lulled into a warm half sleep / half waking slumber. The highway stretched on, mile after mile after mile. It was a straight run for hundreds of miles, only occasionally interrupted by a gas station / convenience store. I glanced over at Amanda who had set the cruise control and then turned it off. She's probably trying to keep alert and not yield to the monotony of the landscape—yellowing fields of wheat or corn or soybeans. Sometimes we'd spot a small herd of cattle lounging in the grass or resting in the shade of a tree or simply cooling off in a a small pond—blissfully unaware of the fate that awaited them:killed, sliced up, and ground up. Maybe we're not that different.

"Sam, you farted. You're disgusting," Mindy blurted out.

"Those who smelled 'em dealt 'em," Sam shot back. ""You're just a big can of bean fart."

"Knock it off," I declared, trying to sound authoritative and immune from flatulence. "Amanda, maybe we need to stop and stretch our legs and go to the restroom."

"I was thinking the same. There's a gas station about three miles ahead. It might be a tourist trap with all sorts of genuine-fake Native American trinkets. We've still got half a tank of gas left, but I don't know how much farther the next gas stop will be." Soon Amanda took a sharp right turn and we pulled up to the gas pumps. Sam burst from the confines of the car and so did Mindy but at a slower more measured pace. Amanda slowly exited the car, a bit stiff from her long stint at the wheel. I got out even slower and started filling the tank. The air felt cooler, even a bit chilly. Off in the distance, a low cloud hung over the mountain obscuring the tops and setting a boundary between two worlds. I joked to myself that the vista was even better than a picture-perfect post card.

I soon had filled the tank, and Amanda blurted out "Your turn." She had broken out into a wry smile. We both knew what that meant: it was my turn to deal with Sam. He would be begging for money to buy some little souvenir of the trip, a memento that he'd soon forget. Mindy would be a bit less blatant in her request and somewhat more selective in her choices. She might want a bracelet or an inexpensive pendant. Maybe she'd settle for some postcards she could mail to her friends back home. She knew better than to ask for too much. If she carefully made an informal cost analysis, she'd fix on something she could get rather than on something that would be denied.

"Dad, take a look at this. It's awesome." Sam had latched onto a four-foot "authentic" Indian spear. I examined it closely, raising Sam's hopes..

Even he had guessed that he had pressed the boundaries of my indulgence. I was looking for two unknowns: the price and the manufacturer.

"Sam, this was made in China."

"So what? It's cool."

"It's also thirty dollars."

"Well, then, how about this?" Sam quickly produced a tomahawk, likewise made in China but with a somewhat lower price tag, twelve dollars.

Sam changed tactics and now gazed upwards at me with puppy eyes— his best approach to begging. Sometimes it worked. This time it didn't.

"Why not try this?" Interrupted a voice, mellow yet authoritative. That voice belonged to a swarthy face that towered above me. This Native American must have been six foot six. He had sharply defined facial features: a large brow, straight black hair that fell past the nape of his neck, deeply dark eyes, a prominent nose, and a chiseled chin. He wore a wool shirt with diamond-shaped patterns of black, white, yellow, and red. His fingers grasped a book.

"Here, take this. It's only four, ninety-five." He looked at me and grinned, "It's not made in China."

Sam eyed the book skeptically. He was probably thinking, "I didn't come here just to be back at school." Still, his eyes turned to the book and fixed on its cover with a bright red thunderbird atop a blazing yellow sun rising above a white, snow-capped mountain. The two-inch base of the cover lay in black with blue diamond-shaped patterns.

Fighting off his aversion to anything resembling school, Sam grasped the book and asked, "May I take a look? The colors are cool."

"By all means, page through it. Look before you buy."

"Hey, there are some awesome pictures of a buffalo hunt and guys with black painted faces with spears and other stuff."

"Yes, but look deeper. What else is there?"

"There's some kind of cool lodge or something and corn fields and fish and —I don't know—maybe beans."

"You guessed correctly."

"There's a lot more in here, too."

"We're not all spears and tomahawks. Killing is easy but living is hard."

I had to confess that I was relieved by Sam's sudden interest. To seal the deal, that kindly but imposing figure introduced himself. "My name's Xavier and for three dollars more I'll throw in a sample of my venison jerky." His lips parted into a wide grin.

"My names's John, Xavier, and you've got a deal." I extended my hand and he grasped it firmly. "Deal."

Sam's face contorted quizzically. "Xavier doesn't sound like an Indian name." Then he broke open the package of jerky, took out a piece, and chewed on it.

"Well, it is and it isn't," Xavier replied as he took my ten dollar bill and gave me the change. "You see, Xavier is a common name in my family. It goes back over four generations when Jesuit missionaries came to our land. So, to my customers and business partners, I'm Xavier. To my brothers and sisters, aunts, and cousins, I'm called Talking Mountain, TM for short. I started talking when I turned two and have never stopped since. My wife tells me that I even talk in my sleep. I go to Catholic mass and to our tribal ceremonies."

"So, you're a little of both?" Sam asked.

"You could put it that way."

Sam still look a bit puzzled, but seem satisfied with that response. "Say, where did you get this jerky? It's some great stuff."

Breaking into a greater grin, Xavier aka Talking Mountain, replied, "I made it myself. Yes, we hunt and kill but only for food, not for sport. Then we harvest the meat and cure it according to our traditional ways. Then we eat it—or, as in this case, sell it to tourists."

Xavier was a good salesman. I sampled the jerky and decided to buy the "bargain" bag for twenty-seven dollars. So, Sam and I both left happy, Sam nibbling away at the jerky and thumbing through his book.

Xavier waved to us as we returned to the car. Mindy had picked out a silver pendant while Amanda had contented herself with a large coffee. "John, I thought you promised that you wouldn't blow money on souvenirs," Amanda stated flatly, neither condemning my indulgence nor praising it. I knew she would even the score in the near future.

Mindy looked at her brother quizzically before she broke her frozen astonishment. "Thank God, you didn't get that tomahawk. I'd never survive the trip."

Sam stunned his sister and parents with his reply. "Killing is easy, but living is hard."

"Where did you get that line?" Mindy asked, a bit astonished at Sam's new perspective.

"From that guy in the shop—Xavier, Talking Mountain, TM for short."

We were almost ready to drive off when TM strode over to our car and hailed us. "Wait! Before you go, I must leave you with two truths. The necklace that the young lady bought—Mindy, right?" My daughter nodded in agreement, intrigued by the sudden interruption. She was accustomed to making impersonal transactions, so she wasn't sure how to handle this striking approach. "Well, here is the first truth. That necklace has great meaning. You know that it's not genuine but only a far less expensive imitation. Still, the value of the necklace and of the pendant has little to do with money. It expresses the beautiful soul of the Navajo people. I am not Navajo, but I admire how they have lived in a land not flowing with milk and honey but a land of sun-baked stones and little water and awe-inspiring sunrises and sunsets. The Navajo have created beauty out of stones. We would do well to do likewise. You are headed to Santa Fe, right. There you can see genuine Navajo creations. While there, take a side trip to the shrine at Chimayo, a little over thirty miles away. There you will also find beauty created from the earth, from sun-baked adobe. You may be astonished at what you will witness."

We shook hands with our new-found guide and revved up the engine and took off. He stood there silently, all six foot, six of him, and as if he were directing us to the right highway. Maybe he was. I suppressed an urge to try to sound clever by quipping some like such as, "No wonder he was called Talking Mountain. He can stand tall and can talk your ear off." But a better instinct told me to keep quiet and accept his guidance. So, we drove off silently. Maybe I realized that Xavier instinctively knew or had learned from years of dealing with travelers that we all were searching for answers to questions we had failed to ask.

So, on we drove, past stone pillars, some brown, some pink. In the distance, snow-capped mountains offered a glimpse into a cooler world. "This is boring," Sam whined. He continued in this peevish mode until Amanda cried out, "Look! Over to the right—a herd of wild mustangs."

It almost seemed as if they were pacing us for a brief span. "Cool," Sam commented. "Wait until we get back home and I can tell my friends." Later, Amanda told me that Mindy had fixed her eyes on the free-roaming horses and turned around to take in a last fleeting glance.

As we turned into Santa Fe, Sam got his fill of cowboy. We had booked a motel at a small, family owned place that was cowboy themed to the max. We stayed in the Annie Oakley Room, where pictures of the famed sharpshooter adorned the walls. Even the lamp stands evoked the mythical cowboy past. The light bulbs shone from the barrel of an upraised six-shooter. Outside our room, just beyond the parking lot, stood an old version of a Conestoga-like chuck wagon. In the small breakfast room, guests could sit on old, worn leather saddles. Here you could feast on beef jerky and beans. Dinner was on your own. Sam chowed down on the jerky and beans. He delivered his verdict. "Cool! Wait until I tell my friends."

We spent one day as many tourists do, frequenting the many shops and art galleries. Everywhere in the midst of a dry, semi-arid landscape bright colors shone. Even the highway overpasses stood out with geometric designs, whose meanings eluded us.

The next day, we decided to follow TM's advice. We headed to Chimayo. Relying on state of the art technology, we got lost—real lost. We ended up in a dusty dead end surrounded by a stick fences. After much fuming and cursing on my part, we managed to avoid the rusty tractor that blocked our way, "You guys headed to the shrine?" Barked out a somewhat bemused voice.

"We got lost following the internet directions." Amanda responded while I sat silent, half-embarrassed and halfway furious. "We must have headed the wrong way."

"A lot of people are," as a man about my height in jeans and plaid work shirt commented amicably as he opened an eight foot stretch of the stick fence that lay on the flanks of the rusting tractor. He grinned as if he were conveying some hidden meaning. I guess he was. "Once you guys get turned around, you need to type in the the Chimayo shrine. That will get you where you want to go. You ended up at the Chimayo pueblo." As we left, he called out, "Adios, que Dios vaya contigo"

"And may God bless you," Amanda replied. Then she turned to me and said, "I was worried we'd be stuck there for hours. I'm just glad he helped us."

"I guess every pilgrimage has its false turns."

In about twelve minutes, we arrived in the dusty, parking lot. A crowd of school-age Indian or Hispanic or probably a mix of both children passed us by as we stopped to survey a fence that from a distance seemed to be made of discarded canes, walkers, and even a few wheelchairs. Just then, a woman clad all in black interrupted our brief reverie. "Yes, it is a charming place. It's on our vacation to-do list. Of course, I don't believe any of that miracle nonsense." Then she stared awaiting some type of affirmation from a fellow gringo. Not receiving the response she wanted, she left. "Well, this is nowhere. Now it's off to see the opera house in Santa Fe. I hear it's a must-see."

The four of us fell into a reverent silence, transfixed by the stark simplicity of the place. Here, the four elements converged: the sparkling, dancing waters of the Santa Cruz river; the brown earth; the blazing fire of the sun; the air and wind just lightly caressing us. Perhaps, this is somewhere.

AND, SO IT'S TRUE

"**A**nd, so it's true," I grimaced slightly—not out of embarrassment as no one was around—but out of the grim finality of it all. I wasn't in the habit of reading obituaries and it wouldn't have made any difference as so many people don't post them any more. I glanced at a brief Facebook posting: Stanley (Stan) Allmen had died. There would be no eulogy, no panegyrics, no accolades, nothing. His remains would be cremated and that was it. Somehow I felt cheated even though I didn't know Stanley Allmen all that well. We had worked together somewhat, but we had maintained a certain distance. Oh, occasionally we'd break tradition and sit at the same table for lunch and we did communicate frequently over email even though our offices were only ten or so strides apart. I had attended his retirement party at the office but so had everyone else at the highly revered Alphabet Soup Enterprises not out of celebration but out of that office ennui. The lunch break would be extended ten minutes. Someone higher up would appear to shake Stan's hand and put on a show that they had become good buddies over the years—even though old Stan had seen the head of personnel only once before and that meeting's agenda had consisted of updating his personnel file, a task that Stan loathed. I know because he had said out loud during lunch to anyone within earshot that he felt the head of HR could have just sent an email and be done with it. "This is all BS," Stan had proclaimed. "This young hire doesn't know what to do with his time. He'll make a note about this 'counseling session.' He gave me that old spiel about how ole TD was like a family. Yeah, it's family, all right. They'll kick your ass out into the street if you seem to cost too much."

But, old Stan's ass was not out on the street. It had mingled with his other remains in some type of funereal urn located, as I later learned, in a closet in his old house. The house had been sold "as is" by some relative from out of state who really didn't want to bother with it. So, I presume the funereal urn was passed onto whoever it was who had bought the house. What the new owner did with the urn and the remains of Stan Allmen I don't know. However, I do know that in some roundabout manner, some distant relative, maybe a cousin three times removed, somehow came to possess the pale lavender vessel of Mr. Allmen.

But, even in death, a morbid sub-genre of comedy prevails. I suppose no one laughed about old Stan's ashes, but the dormant ashes of a distant cousin became the seed for many a family yarn and an occasional muted laugh. The cheap ceramic vessel containing the earthly remains of a distant cousin had spent a fortnight making the rounds of airports. First to Memphis, where one first cousin refused to accept his "gift." Then onto Cleveland, where another "close" relative had it shipped off to Chicago, where an ex-wife lived. She promptly shipped the ashy remains to the deceased's brother who hadn't seen or heard from his sibling in thirty some odd years and had moved to Tucson partially to live as far away as possible from the family he had come to detest.

If all this tale of shipping bears the hallmarks of some urban belief tale, I can assure you that it's no yarn. I know because I was the last to receive the urn and supervised its final resting place. On some gloomy February afternoon, I had opened my mailbox only to discover a small box, tightly wrapped in transparent tape. To open my surprise gift, I had to to employ knife and scissors—perhaps a testament to at least a modicum of familial concern. Wrapped around the lavender urn lay a note scrawled in pen: "Stanley talked of you often, and I'm sure he would like you to locate his last remains in a place of honor." At first I felt chagrined, having no idea what Stan had said about me and no place of honor to rest his remains.I had heard that my former co-worker had served briefly in the US Army and had earned an Honorable Discharge so I checked with the VA rep who assured me that Stan could be interred at the local national cemetery. So, I honorably discharged him to his final resting place. Needless to say, it was a small funeral as I was the only one there. I shuffled about aimlessly and tried to come up with a few final words, but stifled the urge to curse out all of those who had sent the casket—or rather the small urn—packing all over the country. Since I had nothing good to say, I remained silent—except for a one word eulogy, "Goodbye." I don't even know who had paid for the cremation and the urn—perhaps some even more distant relative had provided for those expenses.

As I was exiting the cemetery, a man in mud splattered overalls hailed me. I pulled over and opened the window. He burst out with a somewhat cryptic message:"Hey, buddy, they're oughtta be more guys like you. It would sure as hell make my job easier."

"What do you mean?" I asked, puzzled over what seemed like a compliment.

"You know—I mean disposin' of the earthly remains of your loved one creating or crematin' 'im, you know, and then just sweepin' up the ashes and puttin' 'em in that urn-thing. Makes my job a snap. Instead of having't to dig a six foot hole with some heavy machinery and digging around with a shovel, all's I'd got to do is take out a little auger, turn it a little bit, plop the urn-thing in, and then, 'Voila' as they say, I'm done with the job. And, you know what else? Why we can drop forty or more of the urns-things in the same place as one of them heavy caskets. Saves work and land and money, sort of a burial trifecta. So, thanks, buddy."

Not knowing how to react to the unexpected compliment, I just replied, "Thanks, have a nice day." I drove off, feeling a little ashamed that I couldn't come up with any response other than that cliche. I hit the button to roll up the window and drove off. I wondered why I had even bothered to secure Stan at least the mere shadow of a funeral. Then I reflected on my own impending death and burial. Would anyone bother to show? I recalled a line from a novel I had read in high school, "The spirit gone, man is garbage." Then I linked in another line repeated over and over again, "Garbage in, garbage out." All of this culminating in the monstrous trash heap of humanity. I dismissed these thoughts as just another instance of "Garbage in, garbage out." There would be more work to do.

Cousin It, so named by his ex-spouse, did have a will. None of us would have known about it save for the letter we had received from Morehouse & Sons, Attorneys at Law. There would be a reading of the will in three weeks to dispose of his estate. I couldn't imagine how old Stan could have amassed much of an estate. And in any event, none of his family deserved any portion—however small—of that estate. I balked at first. I wouldn't attend since in life I had little to no interaction with Stan. In death, I had at least provided the semblance of a funeral, but it wasn't much. I even yielded to tradition and decided to abide by family practice and call him Cousin It. So, I'd attend.

The reading of the will was to take place in the concrete and glass confines of the law firm, Morehouse & Sons. There was an underground parking lot to protect clients and guests from the street thuggery going on above. The media had reported a number of muggings in the vicinity and three sensationalized assaults. "If it bleeds, it leads," so I reminded myself. Still, I didn't realize that I'd have to pay for parking—a minor trifle, I guess. I had begun to tally up all of my expenses in this Allmen affair, and felt a bit cheated. Then I despised myself for my greed. Stan's life did deserve at least some form of recognition.

Actually, Stan's vast wealth did receive the recognition denied him in his lifetime. He never married after his first and only wedding—a brief fling that produced no children— never gambled, never drank himself into oblivion as far as I could tell. He went to work, brought his own lunch, and then, I suppose, went home. I don't know when he got up in the morning to prepare for work, but I couldn't help recalling Ben Franklin's aphorism, "Early to bed and early to rise makes a man healthy, wealthy, and wise"—a truth, even if old Ben seldom followed it himself. I parked my car and made sure I had the parking stub securely secured in my rather thin wallet. "Maybe they'll validate the stub and I won't have to pay the two dollar an hour fee for parking in the secured crypt of Morehouse & Sons," I thought to myself. Taking the elevator up to the fifteenth floor, I felt as if I had left a part of me behind. I hoped it wasn't my conscience.

Stepping out of the elevator, I noticed that I could have been stepping into an office site almost anywhere in the country. The same faux oak doors with gold colored nameplates on each private workplace, the same glass windows for the serfs who pecked away at computers, the same tiled floors. In twenty strides, I reached the conference room, where three couples sat and an older man with black hair (probably dyed—it was almost too black to be natural) stood. He sported a black suit with a matching tie. I noticed that his matching dark eyebrows also bespoke the solemnity of the occasion. On the other hand, his tanned face and hands indicated that he must have spent a fair amount of time in the outdoors—probably golfing at some exclusive country club. His trim figure bespoke wealth and health and perhaps a privileged upbringing. Of course, I may very well be wrong. Snap judgements may be snapped in two by time—although I doubt that I would be spending much time with the the three couples who sat stoically

Although the three couples sat stoically, their dress, perhaps I should say their overdress, indicated an excess of anticipated wealth. Perhaps they all knew of Stan's treasure trove. At least, I guessed that he had wealth or why else would we have all have been summoned to a formal reading of his last will and testament? A Zoom session may have sufficed. One couple, too, was tanned like the barrister but the balding man fidgeted constantly as if unaccustomed to his new status while his wife wore a Gone with the Wind outfit with a hooped out lavender dress. To be fair, I admit that the flair of her skirt really wasn't that big. It matched the bulge of her stomach. Then, the couple that sat next to what I assume was the Memphis duo was all decked out in the splendor of Rock star opulence. Deep blue, almost black, jeans contoured to their bodies and star-studded royal blue T-shirt tops. The man had long black hair that reached the nape of his neck; his wife or partner or whatever had a fashionably close-cropped hair speckled here and there with a few streaks of grey. Aging rockers, I guessed. The third couple was decked out in a formality that screamed out, "Just too much." The woman, perhaps in her late fifties or early sixties, exhibited a bloated face that seemed out of place with her tight fitting, sequin studded cocktail dress. It accentuated bulges that best lay covered. The man wore a green tuxedo with a clip-on black bowtie. His neck flowed over the confines of the white shirt. He was a great pains to flash his gold colored, oversized cufflinks. All in all, an orgy of excess. Perhaps they thought that, since they hadn't honored Stan in life, they at least could honor him in death. Perhaps, they may have felt a tinge of remorse for shipping his ashes all around the Midwest. Perhaps—ah, I digress. Idle speculation, just like idle hands, is the devil's playground.

The lawyer opened the reading of Stanley's last will and testament—I believe that's the term—by clearing his throat and checking his watch. Perhaps he was making sure the minutes were included in his hourly billing. Again, I had wandered out into forbidden zones. "I remind you all assembled," he intoned, "that what I will now be saying are the exact words that Mr. Stanley Allmen wrote. So, please be attentive and listen without prejudice against me. These are Mr. Allmen's words, not mine,"

"Just what had old Stan put down in print?" I mused. "The pontificating barrister (or perhaps he's a solicitor—I sometimes overlook the difference) is certainly covering his backside with multiple layers of exculpatory diapers. To my shame, a voice deep within me whispered that during his lifetime Stan had accumulated heaps of money—unknown to anyone else and that he would forego blood kin to bequeath it all to me. But my better half brushed aside that greedy instinct—well, not completely. I still maintained a faint glimmer of hope for the suspected radiance of buried treasure. I guess a part of our nature is pure—or rather impure—pirate.

But, we all soon were informed that Stan's estate was only modestly large. In death as in life Stan remained modest. "To my cousins in Memphis [names withheld to avoid legal implications. Like the leading lawyer, I was covering my backside] I bequeath," the lawyer pontificated, "one fourth of my estate. To my cousins in Cleveland, another one fourth. To my cousins in Tucson, another one fourth. And finally to my colleague at work. I trust that he will accord me some measure of decency in my death as he has in my life." Then the lawyer paused.

It was fairly obvious what the cousins were thinking. "Why is that stranger, that colleague at work, entitled to any fraction of Stan's inheritance? The cousins have rights to a full third, not a fourth, of the estate. Let's see, if the old guy's estate was worth worth four million, as it stands now, we'd each get one million. But, if you factor out the illegitimated claim of that damned colleague, each cousin would get one-third of the four million, a little less than one million four hundred thousand dollars. I mean, a million bucks just ain't what it used to be. Damn that guy. That four hundred thousand could get me that down payment for a luxury place in paradise." All the cousins shot me a dirty look, eyes blazing with envy and a sense of injustice, lips slightly curled in a snarl, just barely repressed.

Finally, after seconds that felt like hours, the cousin from Tucson asked the question that everyone wanted answered. "So, just how much is my dear cousin's estate worth?"

"After deducting legal fees, the estate is worth"—here the lawyer paused solemnly for effect—"five million, three hundred and forty-three thousand, and one hundred and twenty-four dollars, and sixty-four cents."

The whole room remained silent, as ballpark calculations were running through each person's mind. I was no exception. Here is my suspicion of what each person was thinking—the cousins from Memphis had taken out his phone to calculate a bit more precisely. He hunched over in his seat to attempt to conceal what he was doing, but everyone knew. Anyway, here is my rough guess as to what we all were thinking. "Let's see, that's about one million and three hundred and thirty-six bucks, that is if divided by four. Divided by three, it's about one million and seven hundred and eighty thousand bucks. Why that colleague bastard is shorting beloved Stanley's relatives of about one million and four hundred and fifty thousand bucks, that damned cursed colleague." The guy from Memphis had an accurate account: each cousin would get $1, 335, 781. 16 as it now stands; if we factor out the damned colleague, we'd each get $ 1, 780, 000 + bucks. Damn him."

Sensing what everyone was doing, the lawyer broke the silence by pronouncing, "My secretary already has your checks waiting. If you claim your check now, you will have to sign a sworn statement that you have accepted the checks as a full settlement of Mr. Allmen's estate. If you wish to contest the settlement, then you will have to wait for your check." He took a final note of the time by conspicuously checking his watch and marching off.

Even though each party would receive over one and a third million dollars, each person cowered sheepishly and proceeded at a funereal pace to the secretary's office to sign the agreement and, of course, receive the check. No one said a word—including me.

And so ended the affairs of Mr. Stanley Allmen.

What the cousins did with their share of the inheritance, I don't pretend to know. As for me, I'll toast the life of Stanley at his grave and wish him well. With the rest of his money I'd settle a few minor debts and donate the rest to a charity. To which charity, I'd have to do a little detective work So, I guess Stan will live on in that way. After all, it's all true.

A NEW REVELATION OF AN OLD TRUTH

had been sitting here in the cold. Nothing. I thought I was prepared, and maybe in some ways I was. But, I wasn't. Just when you think you see it all clearly, a fog rolls in, some miasma of the mind, I guess.

Yesterday, I thought things were going well. Some friends and I were sitting around a nice fire, toasting ourselves and the memories of what had happened that morning and afternoon. We were all wrapping ourselves in the warmth of success and camaraderie. All was good, so we thought.

Charlie burst out, singing his own praise. "I never thought I'd get him. Last year, I had him in my sights, but he just skittered away. Not this year. I had him dead to rights. Here was that big buck maybe 200 yards away, just standing there, daring me like. I took out my range finder and, yeah, he was 187 yards away."

"Hey, Charlie, you sure you got that right? I was standing there not fifteen yards away, and I'd say you got the 87 right, but you just have tacked on another 100 yards." We all laughed as we knew Ernie acted as our official fact checker. We had to be sure to call him "Ernie" as he hated his given name "Ernest."

"Well, as I was saying, before I got interrupted, that big old buck was just staring me down 187 yards away." Charlie looked around, glaring down the other six in our group. We must have been all thinking the same thoughts: "Just let Charlie tell his own story. He had bagged the biggest buck of the day. Maybe he's earned his bragging rights even if he is embellishing a bit."

"As I was saying before being so rudely interrupted, out there at the crest of the ridge in between two old towering oak trees that had kept their leaves, that old buck was standing there, almost daring me to shoot."

Ernie poked me in the ribs and whispered to me, "That old buck was

PATRICK CONLEY

standing there because he figured Charlie would shoot high and wide to the left, the way he usually does."

Charlie just shot us a glance that all but screamed, "Shut the hell up. It's my turn to do a little chest thumping." So he went on. "So, that buck started moving along the crest of that ridge, not in any particular hurry, I figured. His belly was just bursting with all the acorns he had been chomping. Then he stopped and turned that big ole 12 point head of his towards me. I got him in my sights and then 'Bam.' He stood there a while, maybe wondering what had hit him. Then he eased himself down as if he had known all along that his time had come. He had ruled as king out here, but now I was at the top of the food chain."

None of us said a word. Sort of a moment of silence for the fallen monarch. Even Charlie kept his mouth shut.

Then, surprisingly, Ernie broke that invisible ice that had frozen us in time. "Yeah, Charlie, that was a once in a lifetime moment."

"You're damn right about that," Charlie retorted. "Not everyone gets that."

The next day, I'd have that once in a lifetime moment, but it wouldn't be like Charlie's. Until now, I've kept my mouth shut about it, partially because no one would believe me and partially because I've had to keep churning over just what that moment meant. It wasn't a moment of glory— that I knew. But it was a split second I'll never forget.

Along with Charlie, I and all but one in our group had bagged a buck. At the time, I hadn't thought much about it. My family and I would have plenty of meat for the winter to come even if I shared the harvest with a homeless shelter. I didn't have the bragging rights that Charlie had. Mine was a decent sized buck, a six pointer, and it wasn't near as big as Charlie's. Still it was big enough. I had one more deer tag to fill, one for a doe. Most of the time, we'd just get a tag for a buck, but lately the deer population had swollen. Without any predators other than humans, the deer numbers had exploded. So, all of us would have another day to bag a doe if we wanted. Charlie didn't want to. As he said, "I've gotten more than enough deer, so I'm headed back, but not until I see what you guys can do. I don't want some weird-ass tall tale about somebody besting me." After he left, we all joked that ole Charlie would talk the ears off to as many people who would pause to listen to him gloat. We were placing informal bets on how

46

the story would end up. Soon, some claimed, the twelve point buck would sprout even bigger antlers, bigger than an elk's, in Charlie's yarns. I didn't place a bet. I didn't know and still don't know why I didn't. Somehow it just didn't seem right, spinning a tall tale or joke about the dead.

That night I didn't sleep much. Visions kept me up, dancing in and out of dreams that weren't dreams at all. They seemed too real, but I couldn't exactly define the beings that kept rushing in and out of my mind, not nightmares, but visions of spectral creatures.

"What the hell was eating you last night? We could all hear you tossing and turning like some kind of fidgety squirrel," Ernie blurted out when we gathered at five am for coffee and a breakfast of gravy and biscuits. "It couldn't have been something you ate," Ernie reasoned. "We all had the same supper, beans and barbecued venison. You didn't down any beers or rotgut whiskey either, so that's out. It wasn't what you ate. Something's eating you."

"Ernie, I don't know. I wish I did."

He shot me a glance and, with carefully measured words as he turned away from me, warned me: "Well, you be careful out there. We don't want you to do anything stupid. Did you get enough sleep so you won't doze off or anything in that blind you shoot from?"

"Yeah, I'm good," I responded, a little too loudly. Ernie had his doubts, so did I.

"But I had prepared everything," so I tried to convince myself.

Last summer Charlie, Ernie, and I had come down to our favorite hunting grounds. We cleared brush, trimmed a few tree branches, and prepared the three different spots where we would set up our blinds in the coming fall. My happy hunting ground was located on the top of a "V" shaped ravine. Most of the time, the winds would blow straight into my face. So, I reasoned, if I cleared a small four foot by four foot space, for my future blind, the deer couldn't sniff me. Of course, the winds didn't always blow towards me, but I just had to play the odds. We all worked together to clear the brush and undergrowth. "We sweat our asses off today, so we can fill our bellies in the fall," Charlie would say as he swung his ax to topple a tangled growth of honeysuckle. Ernie didn't say much. He just mowed down undergrowth with his sickle. I carted off the debris and moved it off to the side. Soon, we had cleared two separate spots: one small one for the future blind and another one at the bottom of the ravine where a small creek ran off to the near side and then emptied back underground, beneath a limestone overhang. As I was hauling off the debris, I spotted a small glimmer precisely where the creek took a sharp turn to the right. I don't know why, but I stopped, reached down, and pulled up an old flint arrowhead. "It must have washed down after one of those big July thunderstorms," I thought to myself. Then I shouted out to my co-workers, "Ernie, Charlie, look what I found."

Ernie strolled over, and Charlie paused and just about suspended his ax in mid-air. When Ernie reached out, I handed over the relic. He looked at it, felt the sharp edges, stroked his chin a bit, and concluded. "Well, one thing's for sure. I guess we aren't the first hunters to come here."

Charlie let his steel ax fall without saying a word. Then he ambled over, took a look at the arrowhead, and let out his view in what might have been a joke. "Some guys will do anything to keep from working. Come on, you lazy asses, we've got only four more hours of daylight left." We had already cleared Ernie's area, we were working on mine, and Charlie had drawn the short straw, so we were going to work on his spot last. I let the arrowhead slip into my jeans' pocket. I'd keep it as a good-luck charm.

We did get back to work, and Charlie found that we had more than enough time to clear his area. We also soon learned that we weren't the only predators out there. Swarms of chiggers bit us mercilessly around our ankles, just above the top of the shoe line. Charlie cursed as he yanked off a tick from his arm. One tick must have been on the brush I was carrying over my shoulder. The bloodsucker settled himself at the base of my left shoulder. Ernie pulled off the bloodsucker with a pair of special tweezers he had. We checked ourselves for any more predators that might have been feasting on us. No more ticks. We had disposed of them, but the chigger bites itched for days.

Then on the first Saturday of November, we returned to set up our blinds for the next week's hunt. We further camouflaged our blinds with some of the brush that had sprouted up since August. Then we headed over to a range and sighted in our rifles yet again, headed home, and started packing all that we would need, checked it twice, and then felt a little bit of relief. I even packed that arrowhead I had found—just for good luck. We were ready, so I thought.

On the first day of our two-day hunt, I bagged a six point buck and was feeling proud of myself until Charlie came in with his twelve pointer. I had one tag left, one for a doe. "At this time of year," I consoled myself, "where there are bucks, there are does."

The next morning, about an hour before sunrise, I woke up, showered, and double checked the gear I had set out the night before. "All in order," I reassured myself. "Just as the night before." Ernie and Charlie met me as I walked out of the tent. We wished each other well as we slowly and gingerly took our separate ways towards separate locations. Each of us held our flashlights low to reduce our presence. We all three wanted to be a part of nature and simultaneously apart from it. None of us would admit to a truth we held tightly in mind. None of us wanted to land face down in a pile of leaves and sticks and who knew what else. So, we took our time, or at least I did. In a little over twenty minutes, I could make out the outlines of the blind I had set up a week before and occupied the day before. Setting down my load, I opened the tent flap and cautiously set my equipment in and out of the way. Then, even more cautiously, I stepped in, and prepared for a day of waiting. "But," I thought, "we had planned everything perfectly. Still, you never know exactly what will happen. A doe may or may not make its way within range." It was still dark and the bucks or does must have been treading lightly—it didn't matter and I couldn't tell anyway, as all remained eerily quiet. An owl was calling out its last hoots of the night, another predator, but a nocturnal one. In a few minutes, the blue light of a predawn morning yielded to the bright yellow and orange rays of sunrise. All was at peace.

After a while, a long while it seemed, but then time moved at nature's pace, not mine, a fox squirrel became my temporary companion. Fox squirrels are so named because they share the same pretty auburn fur that a red fox sports.But this particular one may have shared another trait of the fox—its legendary wiliness. This creature, sitting pretty on a branch overhanging my blind, knew I was there. He or she looked at me utterly indifferent. The squirrel knew I posed no threat, so the fellow creature could sit pretty, quite content to munch away at the acorns. The fellow must have spent considerable time munching as his size cast a shadow so large that a casual observer might have mistaken the silhouette for a raccoon's. In any event, I posed no threat, so the foxy creature

49

contented itself with casually munching away at the abundant acorns and occasionally sprinting away to stuff its cheeks with more nuts that he was storing in his vault. "That fox squirrel has more sense than a lot of humans I know—at least he's saving for a future that might be a bit bleaker than the present." I had to confess that I had to include myself in that category of improvident humans.

Then the squirrel dashed off, as squirrels do, perhaps to to find a fresh supply of nuts. Then I was alone. Without much else to do, I took out the arrowhead I had brought along for good luck. At first, I just turned it over in my hand, feeling the sharp edges and then carefully feeling the notches which some unknown hand had carefully made years and decades, and perhaps even longer ago. I held it up to the light of the rising sun and examined it closely. I kept one eye on it and the other one on the meadow beneath me. The stone had been meticulously worked by some skillful and dexterous hand. I could't do that work. "But, then again," I reflected, "there are lots of things I couldn't do. I couldn't make my bullets or my rifle by myself, not even with Charlie and Ernie helping me out. There are so many things I don't know, so many skills I lack, and so much wisdom I don't have. Well, perhaps in time, I may gain some small measure of knowledge skill, and wisdom. Maybe or maybe not." I slid the arrowhead back into my pocket. "What difference does it make?" I consoled myself. "Maybe Charlie's right: we ought to just enjoy being at the top of the food chain. But I'm not Charlie, and I'm not even sure he believes it himself."

Then, I heard a faint rustling on the ridge opposite. Some creature was moving, and it wasn't just a squirrel. I focused my senses as strongly as I could. My eyes strained to see what had made that rustling noise, and my ears strained to hear. Then the noise stopped, and all went quiet. In a few seconds, the rustling resumed, only this time a faint, distant rumbling had evolved into something bigger, like a a huge freight train that suddenly churned into action. The powerful figure came crashing down the hillside. Soon my eyes made out the outline of a deer, but tree branches obscured the upper half of the torso. Was it a doe? I painstakingly leveled my rifle as I had done so many times before. My heart was beating and pounding. I could sense my adrenaline rush but could not hear anything. There was yet another pause. Then in strode the magnificent feature of a buck, its antlers spreading wide and tall.

I couldn't shoot. However, for some mysterious reason, I don't think I would have pulled the trigger even if that majestic deer had been a doe. I eased my finger off the trigger, set the safety, but continued to view the whole scene before me through my rifle scope. Although the buck stood just forty yards away at the farther end of the meadow, the scope drew me in closer. The buck shot me a glances as if to warn me not to intrude. I complied.

Then, completely assured that I was inconsequential, the buck tore into the ground with his right forepaw, the hard hoof tearing up a large divot. He lowered, then raised his antlers. It would be a duel. In strode another buck, accepting the challenge. The two eyed each other, then lowered their heads, and locked antlers. The two opponents hesitated a moment as if waiting for the referee's whistle. Then the grand pushing match began. I quickly checked my watch. It was 10:14. Why I did that, I didn't and still don't know. At first, the buck who had first entered the arena seemed to be losing ground, but he refused to yield more than two feet. The other buck had made his move but couldn't sustain it. Slowly, ever so slowly, a few inches at a time, my buck, the one who had shot me a look of near contempt, regained lost ground. The two unlocked antlers as if following some rules of engagement which I did not understand. Then, as if by mutual consent, the two resumed the match. This time, my buck lost no ground and spent little time defending his rights to the field of honor. He pushed back the intruding buck far off the meadow. The loser sauntered off, perhaps to claim another territory. For now, though, my buck reigned supreme. He wore his antlers as a crown.

The buck again turned his head in my direction, but dispatched me with a chilling air off discourtesy. "Who was this mortal creature who dared to infringe upon my realm?" The buck seemed to be thinking. But, when he turned away, I set my rifle down, no more viewing through the scope, I fixed my eyes in the buck's direction; he stopped and eased his head around, then his whole body. We locked eyes, and for a moment at least, viewed the other as an equal. Then he sprinted back up the hillside he had come down on. Where he went, I still don't know.

I delved into my pocket and took out the arrowhead again. I scrutinized it carefully. Still eyeing it for seconds that seemed eternities, I probed its mysteries. They say that many, perhaps all, Native Americans would honor the animals they had harvested with a prayer that asked for forgiveness and a blessing for the soul of the creature who had entered its new spiritual home. I yearned to be in that home, but realized I could not enter it—not yet at least.

The rest of the day went by slowly, tediously. I had experienced a moment of glory, but it wasn't mine. An hour before sunset, I returned to our campsite without having fired a shot. So, too, did Ernie and Charlie.

"Any luck?" Ernie asked. Both Charlie and I shook our heads.

"Something strange was going on out there today," Charlie commented. "I don't know what the hell it was, but it was weird like. I mean, I think at least one of us would have seen a doe or two."

"Well, I think I'll pay my respects to the buck I shot yesterday," I mentioned.

Charlie turned towards Ernie with a puzzled look, "Now what the hell do you think he means by that?"

"Beats me," Ernie replied. "Right now, I don't think we need to ask."

IT WAS A GRAND AFFAIR

"**I**t was a grand affair," so I thought at the time, "the prelude to a comfortable life of some hard work, but far more self-indulgence." Waiters in black tuxedos and black bowties strolled through the crowded revelers, enticing them with glasses of champagne and tiny plates of hors d'oeuvres—shrimp impaled on tiny golden cutlasses, small sausages wedded to equally small blocks of cheeses. Anyway, I think you've got the picture, extravagant costs without any substance. I don't recall most of the rest of the evening—I was too drunk to remember much of anything that night—but to this day, I wonder just why we were feasting.

Camille—not her real name, I want to shield her from any public shame. That's the least I can do—well, Camille had matched me drink for drink, so I doubt that she can recall much of that evening, either. So, the two of us set our future as drunken sots—perhaps just continuing a lifestyle that we had established in college.

We had met at a fraternity / sorority party in my sophomore year, her freshman. Our curriculum didn't make too many demands on us; neither did our professors. A tacit understanding was reached. They would grant us *A*'s; in exchange, the students would write glowing reviews. In that way, we could party to our heart's content, and they were free to pursue whatever esoteric topic they chose. Our professors wrote articles for learned, erudite journals, and we wrote little or nothing—excluding signing our names for credit card receipts. They had watered down the curriculum (but not their drinks) so that we didn't have to study much and they didn't have to spend much time preparing their students for their future—a hazy future at that, one clouded over in the miasma of foggy hangovers. Anyway, we met, hit it off, and the rest is history, only not a history that either of us had anticipated. Little was expected of us and much was given.

Now, I've been hanging out alone in a an old motel room. The place wasn't built to last, just to make some quick bucks. I took a quick survey of the place. Molded plastic encapsulated the joint—no furniture to move around or just steal, just dingy white plastic spaces that served as tables and chairs. The bathroom, too, was all molded in place. The whiteness of the place must have produced an intense glare, but that was years ago. Now, the whole room just shone dim, with the white plastic glow turned a dull grey—like a wintery February sky. But, I was lucky. I had enough money to pay for a two-night stay where I could shower in tepid streams that flowed over the ingrained dirt and muck of my own body. The toilet worked sort of. I had to pour in water to a tank that had long ceased any pretensions of being white. Now it was darkened with age and cloudy water. Maybe it resembled me. You know, pour in raunchy liquids and look what you get. Still, for two nights I could luxuriate in a room with a bed and get myself semi-clean. After the second night, I was out on my own, in the street.

Most of us hung out in an old alleyway surrounded by reddish-brown bricks that had once housed factories that had been closed for decades. We had to tread lightly because broken glass lay everywhere, so did swirling papers of fast food wrappers. Some of the guys who scored a little money from panhandling would rush out to grab some food at Taco Bell, McDonald's, Burger King, you know all the places. In a frenzy of feasting, they'd just toss the greasy paper or cardboard on the ground, providing food for the local mice and rats who would crawl out of the numerous rooks and crannies of the abandoned buildings to lick off the remnants of grease. The alleyway reeked of the stifling aroma of stale grease along with the piss of half a dozen men. We all did, however, maintain a few remnants of order. If you had to take a crap, you had to open the broken door of the building to the right and do your business in a far corner. You also had to close what was left of a door on your way back.

"Plumbing, you know, is the basis of civilization," I remember Sol telling us. Sol was a guy who once hung out with our small crew, but he had sobered up and now was working at a regular job and going to night school at the same time. In my opinion, he could have taught the teachers. Anyway, Sol didn't come to preach to us. Mostly he just listened. Then he'd make a few suggestions. The first suggestion he made was the poop rule. A young guy—even younger than I was—was bitching about how bad the place smelled. So, Sol said we ought to poop in an out of the way place—not so out of way that it was hard to get to even on legs made wobbly by too much of the sauce and junk. "If you're so strung out that you can't make it to the poop place, then you've got to clean up the stinking pile of shit. It's bad enough to smell your own mess, but it's just shit-worse to breathe in the raunchy stench of someone else's."

So, on Sol's advice, we took our first tiny step towards civilization. But, we were like toddlers just learning to walk. Sometimes we'd stumble and make accidents. Then we had to act like the adults we chronologically were. I had just turned thirty-three, but I knew I had to start learning all over again just how to live.

Sol became my tutor on those Saturday afternoons when he'd come to the place he had graduated from. Only, he didn't deliver lectures. He'd just sit next to me and let me ramble on. Then he'd throw in a comment or two. Sometimes I listened and sometimes I didn't. Sol didn't care. He'd let me go on my way. The next day or the next week I'd think over what Sol had said. In my heart, I knew he was right, but I guess he figured I'd eventually come around, but that eventuality took a long time. No miracle here. Well, maybe there was one. I don't know. Maybe that's what Sol had realized long ago what took me a painful boomeranging of experiences to know. I had to admit that I didn't have all of the answers.

"You know, Sol, I thought I had it all figured out. I presumed that I had done things right. I hadn't, I guess."

"Well, Camille and I didn't have much of a wedding night. I told you before that we had pickled ourselves in juices we couldn't control. The next morning we had to clean up the bathroom where we had retched out our insides. We both laughed it all off. But, you know, Sol, I can still sense that fetid stew of decaying hors d'oeuvres. It's not so funny now. It probably never was.

"After the wedding and honeymoon, which was more like an eclipse where the booze blocked out the sun, we settled down, sort of. We both had jobs, lifetime careers so we thought. First, I'd join the guys for a few drinks after work, Camille did the same, only she joined the girls, or so I thought. We'd both get home late, have a makeshift dinner, and start sleeping it all off. I was a functioning alcoholic. I presumed I could keep on functioning. I couldn't."

A rat scurried out of its fortified castle to sally forth and snatch one of the greasy food wrappers that one of the guys—Jimmy, I think—had hastily torn off to chow down on a something burger. The rat shot us a glance that said, "I won't bother you if you won't bother me." Sol stared down the rodent, who stared back for a second or two and then retreated with his prize, back into the dark recesses of crumbling brick and mortar.

I turned to see what Sol's reaction was. Nothing, at first. Then he leaned back on the broken chair that I had salvaged from a nearby dumpster, turned to me, and said softly. "You know that rat was doing his job, cleaning up the mess that Jimmy or whoever had made. In a sense, he was doing the job that rodents do and taking care of himself in the bargain, sort of a functioning garbage-a-holic."

"Sol, are you saying I'm a rat."

"Naw, you're bigger than the rat."

"Yeah, bigger in what way?"

"That's for you to figure out. Well, I've got to be going. See you next week?"

"Yeah, I'm not going anywhere." For a whole week I juggled over in my mind what Sol meant when he said I'm bigger than that rat.

It took me a while to sort things out, my mind being fogged over and all with stuff I can't even remember. I guess that just shows how meaningless they were—or maybe how meaningless I had become. At last I stumbled over an answer that later I figured out was good enough: I should be better than a rat. I could do a far lot more than scurry in and out of old abandoned buildings where the mortar was so crumbly the bricks just sort of piled on top of each other, like some kind of Jenga puzzle or something. On the highway that overlooked our little rat trap, people would drive by. A few of them would pull over on the shoulder and take a look. They would stop and stare and probably make bets on just how long it would take for the whole pile to just fall all over on top of itself. Hell, they'd probably place bets on the lifespan of the big rats—the people kind—would last, too.

The next week, Sol meandered on over. I think he was letting the bunch of us know—especially Jimmy—that he was coming. You know, so we could clean up a bit before he sat down. This time he was carrying a bag, a big brown grocery bag. We licked our lips in anticipation, sort of like dogs waiting for a treat. Maybe that was a step up from being a rat. He got within shouting distance before he hollered out, "You guys know who's coming and what he's bringing, so set a place for me." It was amazing how fast we cleaned up the place—still a dump but a sort of clean one. Anyway, Sol waited a bit before he got any closer. "I brought you guys some bread. It's day-old stuff, but it's still good. I didn't figure there would be any leftovers." There weren't. We each snatched one of the small loaves he tendered to each of us and chomped down on it real good, time and time again until we had finished it. No scraps, no leftovers. We all thanked Sol, but he wasn't looking for thanks. He looked me square in the eye and said. "Now you know what it takes to be more than a rat."

"I do?"

"Yeah, you do. Think about what I just did."

It didn't take me long to decipher Sol's meaning. The next week when he showed up with his bag of goodies, I whispered over to him," To be more than a rat, you need to shift around your priorities a bit."

"Yeah, how's that?"

"I guess it means taking care of someone else and not just yourself."

"Well, my boy, you finally figured it all out."

"But how do I start doing that? I mean, I don't have any money or anything. I barely get by myself."

"Well, when you were saucing up your brain with booze, what were you trying to escape?"

"Myself, I guess."

"Bingo again, my boy."

"What was Camille doing?"

"The same, I suppose. I don't really know. I was all wrapped up in myself, my career, my dreams, my stuff, my image of myself."

"Yeah, the old my, my, my game. We all get into that at some time or other in our lives."

"But, how do I get out?"

"Well, you can start by apologizing to people you hurt."

I paused for a moment. There'd be too many to count. Sol guessed at what I was doing. "You gotta start small, you gotta start somewhere, but you can't think you'll just win them all over. They probably suspect you're looking for a handout or something. They're dealing with a lot of pain, too, and you know damn well you contributed to that pain. Just start by not expecting anything in return. Start making a little money, work at it, not for yourself, but for the people you hurt. It's not about you, your career, your dreams. You pretty well blew that apart."

I didn't sober up instantaneously or anything. It wasn't like I saw the light and just transformed or something. Sol didn't show for a few weeks. At first I thought that maybe I had offended him or Jimmy did or one of the other guys did. I know now he was giving us time to take those first few steps on very wobbling feet.

I talked it over with Jimmy. He just kept nodding and nodding, then drooling. He was wasted—on what I don't know. That damn rat was eyeing us from the corner. He'd stick out that rodent nose and rat eyes, just waiting to scurry over and devour whatever edible scraps lay on Jimmy's body. I picked up a broken piece of brick and threw it at the hole where the scavenger had hunkered down. But my aim was off and the bit of brick just banged high and broke off in a few shards.

"I guess right now I've got nobody but myself," I muttered out loud. Then I swallowed some pride, lots of it, and feasted on humble pie. When nobody else was looking I shuffled on over to the homeless shelter, where I sat on a bench with other homeless guys, had a cup of coffee and a little bowl of soup. You had to be stone-cold sober there or they'd throw you out on your ass. I did this for three or four weeks. I even got to talking to some of the guys there. Not much of a start, but a tiny step.

Somebody at the shelter, where all of my crew occasionally stopped by for a free lunch, had also given us a phone, not a smart one or anything, but we could make a few calls, only I had nobody to talk with, so it really didn't make any difference. I wondered if Camille still had her old phone number. At least, I remembered that. I debated with myself: should I call her or not. Maybe it would just bring back memories that she'd like to forget. Maybe I was just being selfish. Maybe she'd think I was just begging for a handout. Or, just maybe, I could give both of us closure. Or maybe still it was just all about me. I walked over to a place where the highway noise wasn't so bad. I yanked the phone from my trouser pocket and pecked out numbers I couldn't forget. It was ringing. So she hadn't changed the old number! On the third ring, a deep baritone voice answered, "Yeah, who's calling? What do you want?"

"I just wanted to say, 'I'm sorry.'"

"Yeah, we all screw up from time to time. No problem, buddy." That was it. Nothing more.

I think deep down, I yearned to hear Camille's voice. I guess I was still obsessed with me. She had probably moved on. I had just moved down. That voice that had answered me calmly might have been her boyfriend, her new husband, or maybe just some guy who had randomly been assigned her old number. It had been a couple of years. Who knows how long that has been? When I used to say, "I had only a couple beers," that could have meant anywhere between two and twenty-four. "A couple of years" might have meant anything or nothing. It was time to move on.

With no place to go and no one else to talk with, I shuffled on over to the homeless shelter about four blocks away. This time, though, I couldn't just sneak and quietly take my coffee and soup. I'd have to beg.

"Need a job," I mumbled, staring blankly at the floor.

"What? I can't hear you," some nameless volunteer answered.

"I need a job," I replied with my eyes still downcast.

"Well, let's start over. My name's Doug. We can't pay you now. You still want some work?"

"Please, I just need a job."

"Well, you can start back in the kitchen and get those dishes washed."

When I was a kid, doing the dishes had been one of my chores, and I hated it. Now, however, the sheer boredom of it all somehow seemed relaxing. It wasn't much, but at least I was doing something productive. When I finished with the dishes, I looked in a dingy closet and found a mop and a bucket and started washing the grimy and greasy floor.

"Hey, buddy, you trying take my job?" cried out that nameless voice. Or, maybe it wasn't nameless.

"Hell, no, Doug, right?" He nodded. "I was just looking for something to do."

"Yeah, well, your pay is the same as mine—nothing, at least no money. While you're on this cleaning binge, how about scrubbing the toilets?"

I wasn't sure if he was testing me or what. For some reason, I blurted out, "Sure, no big deal." So off I went.

In about half an hour, Doug came back. It wasn't an inspection or anything. He just looked at the bathroom and commented in a deadpan voice, "Since you got that all cleaned up, you may as well clean yourself. Here's a towel and there's the showers." Those warm streams of water washed away more than dirt.

I kept working there for maybe three months. Then I started getting paid. I found a room in the shelter where I could stay for a while until I found a higher paying job. Sol would come in to see me and he always said,"You've made yourself more than a rat, you know."

In nine months, I found myself becoming Sol. It wasn't easy. And sometimes I just yearned for a drink. It wasn't like I just had a craving. Something was pushing me off the cliff into some boozy ocean. I did fall off once. Sol was standing over me. "Hey, rat, you're lying in your own stink. Go take a shower and I won't tell the super what happened. I could see it coming. You just tuned everybody off and went staring off into the cloudy mists of your own mind. You were thinking, 'I just gotta have a drink, just one.' But you know what they say, 'one drink is too many and a hundred ain't enough.' By the look and stench of you I'd say you were way the hell over one cup of poison. It wasn't pretty."

When I had sobered up, I had to apologize to Sol. He replied, "That's not enough. You got to apologize to yourself and a few other folks."

"You mean the super, the guy who runs this place?"

"Bingo, buddy. He can figure out what happened last night. Just about everyone can. You admit to him that you screwed up."

"But what if he tosses me out? I got no place to go, nowhere to live."

"It's a helluva lot more likely that he won't throw you out if you got the guts to admit you're sorry. This road trip doesn't go in a straight line, pal. It's got twists and turns and, yeah, sometimes dead ends. Sometimes you got to throw it in reverse and back out of a bad situation."

So, once again Sol had saved my ass. I cleaned up, went to the super, expecting the worst. All he said was, "Just don't let it happen again." I didn't.

I had to mull things over. I threw myself down on my cot It creaked but didn't break. "No, I didn't have all of the answers, maybe none of the answers. I've got to think beyond myself." After a while, maybe just three minutes or so, I could look out and see a vast scroll unrolling a little at a time—sort of like ocean waves just slowly rolling onto a far shore. Only the waves weren't water but people, all sorts of people holding hands so no one broke free and crashed against the rocks. Maybe when Sol was saving me, he was also saving himself. I've seen that same look in his eyes—calm, placid, reaching out to me and others.

In six months, I was making enough to splurge a little. So, I went over and brought the guys I had hung with some sandwiches, foot long hot salami sandwiches. One of the guys—not Jimmy, he was too far gone—started a little fire to boil water. Sol brought some cups and some hot cocoa mix. It was a grand affair.

FOREWARNINGS

"**A**-I, robotics, a world without work, not a worker's paradise but a pleasure palace of delights. I can envision it all now You want a steak cooked medium-rare, and in ten minutes or even less your meal is ready. You want a little soothing background music to provide some ambiance and you've got it. Hell, we've got that now. You don't have to deal with stubborn, mulish, and recalcitrant servants or workers; you just have to have your personal robot fulfill your every need. It's almost too perfect. So, Dan, you've been quiet all this while. So, just what do you think?"

"Someone will have to repair the robots and someone will have to develop the algorithms for the A-I. Looks to me as if we've got a world divided into classes, the perfect storm for class warfare."

"Dan, you're not just a Luddite; you've got some weird dystopian mindset. Come on, you've got to admit that the techno world has made life better. Even middle class people enjoy luxuries that only medieval kings and queens could savor while the working class broke their butts hauling manure and cutting wood, and dying in constant battles over land—which meant wealth. And the wealth would belong only to the upper crust. For your ordinary worker, life is much better now than its was even three generations ago.'

"I'll grant you that much, maybe even more, Joe. It's true that the work—such as it is—isn't back-breaking, just soul and mind-breaking. We dispense drugs like candy. Your old buddy, Karl Marx was said to say, 'Religion is the opiate of the people,' or something pretty close to that. Now we throw out pot and other drugs like candy to the cheering crowds. We've got almost half of the population stoned out."

"Dan, where the hell have you been? Nobody starves. Hell, they just overeat. Don't we have an obesity crisis. We've got three-fourths of the folks on weight loss drugs. You want food—you've got it. You want booze—you've got it. You want to get stoned on your ass—you've got it. You want sex—you've got it. We've got a workers' paradise without work. It's the best there's ever been. It's just one big joy ride."

"Joe, where have you been? Have you seen the other side—the side where most of the people spend their lives. Now that's a hell-hole."

"Dan, why should I go there when I can get everything I want here? I mean some days I work long hours, but I'm amply rewarded. Side trips to a nearby resort where I can order up anything I want—booze, sex, whatever. Then there's the vacations to island paradises: warm sun, blue skies, cool breezes to caress me while I lounge in a hammock on pristine sand beaches within thirty yards of gently rolling waves and water just cool enough to make you want to dry off in those sunny rays. What a life!"

"Joe, you've got a point, but still something's missing."

"Dan, what the hell! Do you want to live forever or some bullshit like that?"

"Joe, just go with me to visit the other side."

"You're kidding, right?"

"No, I'm for real."

Joe rubbed his chin, and slowly, weighed his words. "All right, you've got a deal, but only if you take a bet."

"Sure, Joe, I'm game. So, what's the bet?"

"OK, Danny-boy, here's how it goes. You've got three days to prove to me that this workers' paradise—without really working—isn't the best there's ever been. You just show me that we haven't created the most perfect society there's ever been. You do that and you can enjoy the sweet love of the best sex-bot that's ever been. You can have Dahlia for a week of paradise, buddy. Hell, I'll charge 'er up to the max and program her for delights you've never known. I know you won't win, so I can offer the moon, Danny-boy."

Dan paused for a moment. Then, Joe broke the silence. "So, what do you want if you win?"

"Just watching you feast on Humble Pie for the rest of your life would be reward enough."

"It's a deal. But, you can forget the whole Dahlia thing. You're right.

The winner gets the loser to stuff himself with Humble Pie. But I won't need three days. Three hours will be enough."

"All right, Danny. The bet's on. You've got three hours to prove me wrong."

The two shook hands to seal the deal. Dan then left. So did Joe, but the two went separate ways.

On a deliberately slow walk home, Dan weighed his prospects for winning a bet that just amounted to a sophomoric game. "No matter who wins, it won't change anything. Joe will still find his true love with a mechanical toy, and I'll still be brooding over a system I can't fix.. Still, for some silly reason, I want so much to win if only to have someone else to share my thoughts and refine them in the process."

Dan was right. The system was in place and welded onto the foundation of the entire system. Five classes of people lived out their lives—such as they were in the workers' paradise, aka The Agency. Tier One players—everybody had become a player—consisted of those who had excelled in school, and imbibed every precept from teachers, supervisors, and everyone else with an Elite Players (EP) rank. Anyone who had qualified for the Elite Player cohort could anticipate a life with the best food, the best accommodations, the best sex, and a life of luxury never before experienced by mere humans. Perhaps, they had metamorphosed into demigods. But they had to pay a price: they worked long hours to ensure that the lower tiers were content. Tier Two players, aka Average Players (AP's) had done well in school but lacked the refined finish of the Elite Players. Perhaps to console himself with his reduced status in the Agency's game, Dan sometimes toyed around with a possibility. Maybe the so-called Average Players had been assigned their reduced status because they questioned some of the Agency's decisions. In theory, Tier Two players could prove their worth and move up to the status of Elite Player but that seldom—if ever— happened. Dan had doomed or redeemed himself to Average Player status by openly questioning the free drug dispensary policy. "The open access to drugs keeps Tier Three and Tier Two players content, more malleable to the Agency's infrequent demands," Dan had been advised. He mulled over the response to his concerns and thought only to himself: "Yeah, right, every generation or so the robot warriors can't finish the battle, so the Agency throws in a little cannon fodder." The Elite Players could read Dan's mind.

The Tier Threes were entitled to as much mind-numbing booze and pot as they could stomach, a minimum of four wall-to wall TV screens in their apartments They could work—but seldom did—a maximum of twenty hours a week. The rest of the time they could devote their energies to smoking tobacco and / or pot. Or, they could drown themselves 24-7 with Agency propaganda on at least one of the four TV screens. Frequently, they would venture forth from the confines of their living space to resupply their allotment of drugs, but otherwise they could expect to live out their lives until age forty-eight, so the Agency determined. However, many of the Tier Threes had already overdosed on drugs or otherwise impaired their health so that they never reached the Final Solution—but more of that later. Those who had managed to survive—but only barely—descended into Tier Two states, where they consumed voluntarily or otherwise so many drugs that they quickly achieved their own Final Solution.

The Tier Fives were another matter. The Agency had designated them as Fringe People. They lived outside the boundaries of politely designated society. In mountains and hills and deserts and tundras they barely maintained a subsistence existence. Still, they had insulated themselves from the Agency's domination. Of course, the Agency could devote the energy and resources to eradicate this pesky group, but the Tier Fives were just mere pesky flies in this garden of earthly delights. They had their freedom but not much else.

Dan strolled into his apartment. Tier Four players could dispense with the wall-wall-TV screens if they wished but had to present proof of having devoted at least four hours a day to listening to the Agency's broadcasts.

"Maybe, just maybe, Joe's right. We could have it a helluva lot worse," Dan reflected. Then he quickly chose his meal: freshly grilled salmon and asparagus along with a small baked potato garnished with parsley and sprayed with a non-fat artificial butter spray. While Dan waited for his order to be cooked—he had only seven or eight minutes to kill—he savored a vodka martini, stirred but not shaken. He took a small sip. "Maybe Joe's right. I have what I need and far more. Hell, I'm even exempt from the Final Solution—at least for the time being. In six minutes, not even seven, Dan feasted on his chosen fare. He could even knock off some time from his required viewing time. The Agency's news broadcast featured an account of drones and robotic warriors annihilating the Agency's foes in far off lands that few—if any—had ever heard of. Still, these accounts kept the masses entertained and fearful enough not to cause any trouble. There was a risk—albeit slight—that some of theTier Threes might be drafted although few could pass the physical requirements. Dan sipped on his martini, "Maybe Joe's right," he reflected. "Maybe I should just admit defeat, and let Joe win the bet before I risk slipping into Tier Three or even lower status."

But then the TV screen blared out a news flash: "The enemy has capitulated and is ceding more land to the Agency. This might be the time to rejoice and party on." The newscasters had long since ceased being human. A-I created images of smartly clad men and women with hair so perfectly sculptured to fit the artificial faces of perfectly designed faces. Beauty had been scientifically studied down to fractions of a millimeter: the length, color, and texture of the hair; the breadth of the forehead; the length, arch, texture, and color of the eyebrows; the color of the eyes matched to the color of the skin; the length and alignment of the nose and chin; the length of exposed neck and upper body. The Agency had created its own projection of beauty but one not limited to one race or body size. Since the journalists functioned simply as mouthpieces for controlling powers they could all come in different sizes and features. Dan had correctly guessed the inhumanity of the TV images; his Tier Four education had only confirmed his insights.

Dan slowly put down his drink. He hadn't even sipped half of it. "To hell with this," he said under his breath. The Agency might be listening, but probably not. Dan realized that so far he had been nothing other than a model of Tier Two behavior. Huddled over a piece of paper, he scrawled out notes to himself that read: "Two visits needed 1) Tier Three bungalow; 2) The Drop Spot." He tried to suppress a grin breaking from his pursed lips. "That's it," he thought to himself. Then he called Joe from his wrist-phone, purposely using outdated technology because the Agency no longer bothered itself with checking on outdated technology that only Tier Fives might use. "Joe, meet me tomorrow afternoon at two o'clock. I'll be at Area 46 in the Grey Zone, Apartment 87—but the actual apartment number is immaterial. It's all the same."

Joe shot back. "That's Tier Three territory. Aren't we a little old to be slumming it."

"Just meet me there at two o'clock. If you want, you can select the specific apartment number. It won't make any difference They're all the same."

"So, this is how you're going to win the bet?" Joe had lapsed into sarcasm.

"Maybe. I've got a backup plan in case this one isn't enough."

"I'm game. The die is cast."

The next day at the appointed time and place, Dan almost bumped into Joe as he turned the corner past the local dispensary. Every neighborhood had a dispensary. Customers didn't have to pay, but they did have to register and record their "free purchases." Each neighborhood dispensary dished out free pot and and all of the munchies the Tier Threes could handle. Take too much for several months and you might end up a Tier Four; not take too much and your motives might be questioned. Still, it was unusual, but not suspicious, for Tier Two's to be visiting Tier Threes. They might have relatives there, the Agency maintained, and besides, sometimes it was good for Tier Two's to be reminded just how good they have it.

"OK, Joe, you pick—any apartment you want. As I said, it won't make any difference."

"All right, how about number 78. I've inverted the digits as just a safeguard— no preplanned set ups."

"No problem, they're all the same."

"So, Dan, why this area?"

"I used to reprogram cleaning robots around here, so I got to see places before they were sanitized."

The two gingerly stepped down into the maze of underground apartments and gently pushed open the half-closed door to Number 78. Cardboard pizza boxes, some with euthanized rodents still in them, slowly rotted and tainted the air, like the stench of death itself. A reeking mound of other Tier Three munchie-orgies was festooned with candy wrappers, scraps of fast-food hamburgers and tacos and smashed paper and styrofoam cups, some with vestiges of some dubious sickly-yellow liquid oozing out of the smashed remains—a rancid and fetid interior landscape. A man, perhaps in his mid-thirties lay on a sofa, his head thrown back, his mouth agape, his arms, thin and singularly lacking any musculature whatsoever, and his stomach bulging out from under a white tee shirt. His belt lay unbuckled. Perhaps, he had become fully aware that it could no longer contain the multiple rolls of fat that pushed ever outward. He lay there barefoot and barren of any purpose. A naked Tier Three woman snored in the adjacent bedroom, completely naked. Perhaps the couple would awaken for some amorous coupling and then pop a few HHP's (Happy Harmony Pills) that they had picked up, free of charge at the local dispensary. The Agency would grin and approve. Besides, in an hour or two, robotic cleaning services would tidy up the place to prepare for another day in paradise.

"Well, Dan, I got it, but you still haven't completely won me over. I mean, it's not all like this, is it?"

Dan didn't respond but simply directed the two upstairs. Back on the street, Dan walked over to the Tube, a high-speed subway system that would take them out of the Tier Three Zone, Past the Tier Two zone, and end at the boundary of the Tier One's expanse. On the ride, Dan turned towards his somewhat dazzled companion and asked, "How are your shoes?"

"What the hell are you talking about, Dan? What's with the 'How are your shoes'?"

"We'll need to walk uphill over stoney terrain about two miles to the Drop Zone."

"The Drop Zone, huh? Well, I've heard muffled whispers about the place but never been there."

"Well, if you liked the glimpse of Tier Three life, you'll just adore the Drop Zone."

Joe and Dan said not word on the short trip on the Tube. Soon, they seemed to be belched out at the end of the line— a patch of dried mud with overgrown brambles and burs. The wind carried a rancid odor of decaying flesh. "Well, Dan, you sure know how to pick a vacation spot," Joe barked out. "How far do we have to trudge through this shit-hole place?"

"Two miles. It's flat for about the first mile. Then we walk uphill over a terrain of loose limestone and shards of flint. You can see the top of the hill in the distance."

"Yeah, well, right now all I can see are the burs on my pants. And that stench! Is there any way to get rid of it?"

"It's part and parcel of the ambiance, Joe. You'll get used to it. Most people do."

When the two had cleared the brambles and burs, Joe looked up to the top of the hill, nudged Dan and asked, "What the hell are those things?" He pointed to what at first appeared as a flight of helicopters circling the crest of the hill.

"Those are VD's, Joe?"

"Yeah, so what are VD's?"

"You'll see. Just wait."

So, on they trudged. When they reached the crest of the hill, they gazed down into an abyss of rotting flesh and what appeared to be red marbles.

"So, Dan, now I've got an idea of just what the *D* in *VD* stands for—just some big-ass drones."

"And the *V*, Joe, what's your take on that?"

The drones are dropping something into that huge pit. Oh, hell, they're dropping bodies, naked human bodies into that pit."

"And then what, Joe?"

"The drones descend, fold their wings and with what looks like beaks, pluck out the eyes. Oh, now the human eyes gone, these robotic vultures start tearing into the cheeks and jaws. What the hell are they doing, Dan?"

"They're looking for gold teeth, crowns, inlays, whatever is of value. They're programmed to do that. Nothing is wasted. The Agency sees to that. And no need to ruin decent parkland with pointless cemeteries that no one goes to anyway."

"Then what, Dan?"

"The plucked corpses are laid on a conveyor belt on the far side of the pit. You can see the opening from here. Then the remains, such as they are, are ground up into fertilizer and / or pig food. As I said before, nothing is wasted. The end product of a workers' paradise."

"All right, Dan, you win."

FOUR MINUTES

"Y ou have four minutes."

"Only four?"

"Well, that's the norm and the one that most of our clients prefer. Of course, you may have a few more if you select option B. I wouldn't advise that choice. It only prolongs the inevitable and results in unnecessary discomfort. And, of course, we all want the process to proceed smoothly and without any frivolous delays. Really, it's in your best interests and we do have your best interests at heart."

"I see. I appreciate your concern. Then option A it is. Do I still have four minutes before you begin?"

"Of course, the clock doesn't start until you make the final choice. And you have two more decisions to make. We try to allow our clients as much choice as possible. Once again, I advise you to take the slightly more expensive option. For only pennies more, you can select the upgrade; and, when I say pennies, I mean literally only $1. 35. This option guarantees almost instantaneous completion of the procedure and avoids any other tedious side effects."

"Well, you seem to have thought of everything."

"Oh, I have several years of experience in the field, and I have learned one thing above all else: the client deserves the best, for this is a once in a lifetime experience. So, I'm assuming you are choosing the upgrade?"

"Yes, but, How do I—"

"We have your credit card on file. In fact, we have quite a bit of data on file about you. Don't fret. We are guaranteed payment, and you will have no more worries. Now, your final option is to select one of the following three positions: standing, sitting, or kneeling."

"Which one do you recommend? I mean, I've never done this before."

"Sitting is more comfortable for you and ensures that no accidental twitches will interfere with the process. Sometimes, clients wobble a bit standing, and kneeling often results in swaying. There's no difference in price, so sitting is the way I'd go."

"Well, I must say that you have done a fine job of guiding me through the process."

"No thanks needed. I'm just doing my job. The whole business has become rather routine, you know. Over the years, I've guided countless clients like you through this most difficult process. So, please review the following options: You've selected option A and the upgrade for an additional fee of $1.35."

"Yes."

"And you have also chosen the sitting position, right?"

"Yes."

"Very well, then. The clock starts now. For an additional fee of $5, you may order the cocktail of your choice. For $5 more, you can relish the moments with a top shelf brand. Many of our clients select a single malt Scotch on the rocks, one that they can sip slowly for the full four minutes."

"Yes, the Scotch sounds refreshing."

"Then, your complete bill comes to $11.35—ten dollars for the last sip so to speak and one dollar and thirty five cents for the upgrade, a real bargain and one that your whole family will appreciate. A small price to pay for that once in a lifetime experience."

The minutes and even the seconds wound down slowly. The client sipped his Scotch with a resolute intensity.Then the server brought out a covered silver platter and set it noiselessly on a stand. The executive server—Will, for that was his name—positioned himself precisely behind the head and neck of the client to reduce the blood spatter on himself. Will recalled his first few days on the job. One of the first things he learned was that the correct term is *spatter*, not *splatter*. But that was years ago and hundreds of jobs ago. The clock was still flashing down the seconds and minutes in a brilliant red. It was stationed out of the sight line of the client, slightly behind him or her but within the range of the executive server's peripheral vision. Three minutes and nineteen seconds remained.Will still had some time before he uncovered the silver dish that lay before him. For a minute he gritted his teeth. "Come on," he reflected. "It's almost time.

Let's get it over with." This was his fourth job of the morning. When it was over, he could sit down to his lunch, stretch a bit and, perhaps, if time remained, take a brisk walk before he returned to finish his afternoon appointments He gazed at the back of the head of his client. "Well, at least this one accepted his fate graciously," Will reflected. He recalled some of the messy jobs during which the client thrashed about or begged piteously. He hated to have to restrain the individual and tie the distraught client to the chair. One time he even had to incapacitate a victim by capping him first. Not only was kneecapping a messy affair, but his supervisors had to charge his family additional cleaning fees and charges for the additional bullets. Will shook his head. "But this one seems to be a nice fellow—very gentlemanly and stoic."

Will glanced again at the red clock, just two minutes and eleven seconds remaining. Still, it was time to lift the cover and inspect his tool, a semiautomatic .45 Colt revolver. "This will do the job, best. When clients chose the base model—a .22 revolver—sometimes it would take two shots to finish off the job if the client twitched a bit or futilely tried bobbing or weaving his head." He inspected his tool; he had a full magazine if he needed more than one bullet, but he felt assured that only one would do. He glanced over at the clock. Less than a minute remained. He held the pistol with two hands firmly, slowly raised it, and fixed his eyes intently at that small spot just above the nape of the neck. Now the red lights of the timer were flashing. Almost time. 10-9-8- Soon it would all be over and Will could take a break and have his lunch. He fired and it was over— minimal mess and no problems, just a routine day at work, so it seemed.

Will unloaded the pistol and carefully placed it and the magazine back on the silver plate and covered it. He noticed the empty glass of Scotch. "Well, he finished it," Will observed. His assistant would clean up the mess and a drone would come and pick up the body and deposit it in the crematorium just a few hundred yards from the processing center.

Despite being hungry, Will didn't saunter over to the break room. Instead he took slow, measured steps. "That last fellow—I never did get to know his name—took it all so stoically, so gentlemanly. In another context, I could see myself siting down with him and sharing a drink. What had he done?"

Will reflected on his seventeen year career with the Special Services

(SS). "At first, we dealt with serial murderers, rapists, and drug dealers. They were a mean lot, and most of the time we would just tie them to a post and have a firing squad dispose of them, five shooters with only two of them having live rounds and the other three firing blanks. The thought was that none of the firing squad would know who had actually killed the client. But they knew. Then Special Services started using black powder rifles so that there was so much smoke that the squad members really couldn't tell who had fired the mortal shot. Special Services (SS) soon had to deal such a volume of clients to be executed that SS quickly abandoned that approach. It was just getting too costly. Then SS began charging the immediate family of the client the cost of bullets and powder, but that proved to be a bookkeeping nightmare, and some families balked at the idea as the costs kept mounting. So, the SS invested in a carefully crafted in-service program to instruct Executive Servers how to dispose of clients efficiently with minimal costs to the family of the client.

"The carefully constructed course consisted of instruction in conflict mediation—calming down an emotionally distressed client, spatter analysis with live rounds, and, of course, detailed instruction in how to correctly fill out and submit the requisite government paperwork. "Very few acknowledge just how time-consuming it is to submit the forms. There are sixteen of them: billing forms for the bullet and additional cleaning fees if necessary, confirmation of disposal, the original confirmation of the order of execution, the signed witness attestation of the Executive Server and the Assistant, photographic evidence of the end result, et cetera, et cetera. Blah, blah, blah." Filling out the forms was more tedious and irritating than doing the actual job.

Still, for once, curiosity got the better of Will. "You know," Will found himself talking out loud to no one but himself, "that last fellow seemed a decent sort—maybe like me some eighteen or twenty years ago." He slowly and deliberately walked at a funereal pace to the break room. He paused before he extended his ID badge to be scanned in entry. Then he asked himself a question that he hadn't asked himself for years, maybe even decades: "Why?"

For the most part, Executive Servers ate alone, so none of the thirteen or so other workers took notice of Will sequestering himself in a distant corner. He found himself chewing something—he had forgotten what. "I guess I fixed myself some type of vegetarian sandwich. It doesn't matter." He returned to his prior thoughts. "Why? Twenty years ago, this job didn't exist. But then mobs of red-eyed assailants would circle around vulnerable victims—the elderly, the disabled, the young, the weak—yank their victims to the ground and then pound their heads mercilessly on the unyielding concrete pavement. Other crowds would ransack stores, especially luxury ones, and snatch whatever they could carry off. Corpses lay unburied on the street. Sometimes half-drunken or drugged gangbangers would douse the lifeless bodies with gasoline and set them on fire. People were scared to go anywhere and isolated themselves in barricaded houses or apartments, just waiting for the hordes to attack. But then things changed. For the better, I guess. Maybe not."

Will finished whatever it was he was eating. He leaned back in his chair, nodded to a few other Executive Servers also sitting alone in remote corners of the break room and then returned to his thoughts. "But things are better, so we're told. No more gang violence—many of them had been terminated in the first five years of the Service. Then people cheered on the Executive Servers, hailed them as heroes of the State, lavished them with praise, paid them generously, and supported lavish pensions for them. In three more years, I'll have my pension—ninety percent of my highest annual wage. Maybe work for a few more years in some other job, make more money, and wouldn't have a care in the world."

But not even the promise of a relaxing retirement could entice Will into accepting his future life of ease and comfort, even relative luxury. His hand was shaking as he drank of cup of coffee that he didn't even remember pouring. "That last client—I never knew his name—it's better that I don't, at least better for me—. He was such a nice guy. He accepted his fate—a State ordained fate—stoically. As far as I know, he wasn't a criminal, I don't think. What was his crime? Back in the old days of the Service, I didn't have any qualms about disposing of rapists, murderers, drug dealers. I mean, the job was tough physically. We had to restrain thrashing arms and legs as the client was cursing and spitting at us. But spit washes off. So does blood. I recall one guy who must have sharpened his nails before he was to be serviced. He ripped my right arm with nails as sharp as filleting knife's. I had to call in for an assistant just to help me tie him up standing on the post. My assistant had to tackle his thrashing legs so I could bind them tight. All the while the client screamed, "Fuck you, fuck you, fuck you. Go to hell, you bastards." Soon he didn't scream obscenities or anything else, for that matter.

"But now, the clients were different. They just didn't accept the party line. Yeah, we had disposed of the worst criminal elements. But that alone just didn't satisfy the ruling class. They wanted a perfect world where they could be waited on by mindless, loyal minions, catering to their every whim." Will found himself talking out loud, but quietly, so he thought. His thoughts drifted back to his schoolboy days—days before whoever it was that now had power. He recalled the ominous absurdities of the Orwellian world: "War is Peace"; "Freedom is Slavery"; "Ignorance is Strength." "Yeah," said just a little too loudly, "We're ignorant all right. We don't even know who rules over us, makes the grand pronouncements, none of that. 'It's for your own good,' so the government TV sponsored television news anchors tell us, with those pasted on smiles. Hell, for all I know, those newscasters may be robots, programmed by God-knows-who. Who does make the decisions anyway? The government, but who is the government? Rule by committee, that's what it is. But, who forms that committee? The Committee, wasn't that what Ralph Ellison wrote about. Yeah, the Invisible Man and the Invisible Committee. They planned the riots at the end of that novel. Only now in real life, some anonymous, invisible committee planned not just a short-lived riot but a long term criminal rampage—one that would be followed by the inevitable cry for stricter laws and harsher, immediate punishments for, after all, Freedom is Slavery when we're all imprisoned in our own homes, double-bolted locks and security cameras on every corner and, for those who could afford it, every home. Maybe it's time I retired—you know, a kind of self-imposed exile." He looked up at the clock and at the emptying break room.

When his lunch break ended, when the room was cleared of everyone but himself, four Executive Deputies strode into the room and circled Will. "Come with us," bellowed the sergeant in charge. "It would be best if you came quietly."

"But, what of my afternoon clients?" Will stammered.

"We've already taken care of that. Your assistant will take your place. As usual, we've taken care of everything. You haven't a choice in the matter. You never have."

Will stood up obligingly. "These guys are just doing their job as I did for years. I hope I pass with the dignity and grace of my last client." So, Will went off with his escort. He would be added to the afternoon disposals. All turned out well: the State wouldn't have to pay his pension and his family would owe less than thirteen dollars to take care of an aging member.

A FRAZZLED AND FEEBLE
AND FRAGILE FINISH

"It was a frazzled and feeble and fragile finish," the announcer boomed out over the PA. The crowd seconded the conclusion by rushing to the exits twenty minutes before the match ended.

The announcer's words echoed in Danny's mind, bouncing again and again against his skull. Danny had long since abandoned excuses. He had run out of them. "Yeah," Danny admitted, "we got beat in every way imaginable." That realization drove the painful dynamic of failure even further. Danny sat down slowly, easing himself into a self-revelation. "I've no one to blame but myself," he confessed in darkness and isolation. Alone in the clubhouse, he had observed that his players had rushed to the exits even faster than the fans had. Pouring himself a double Scotch, he sipped it slowly.

"Three years ago, only three years ago, I was the toast of the town," Danny comforted himself. "The headlines read, 'The Man Who Defies Time.' That was the glory year. I could do no wrong," Danny boasted to no one but himself. "At seventy I could keep pace with the best of them, so the news accounts had it. But they were all lies." This time the sips of Scotch had mutated into one long draft that emptied the glass. "I wonder if all the news just amounts to one long exercise in deception. Even then I could barely keep pace with the young players for more than a stride or two. Still the headlines ran with the line, 'The man who defies time.' Yeah, the sportscasters feasted on that theme for a while. It made for good press, you know, perpetuating the myth of eternal youth. Well, whatever youth I had has spent itself." Danny looked down at the empty glass and saw just a glimmer of his furrowed brow and thinning white wisps of hair.

"I guess I'll have to tell Emma the truth she probably already knows. The long run is over after all these years. She'll miss her role as a surrogate mother to the players who, for the most part, are younger than our two children. Emma would comfort and console boys who were making more money than their fathers ever had or, for that matter, more than I ever had earned. One gifted young man, really just a boy of sixteen—Robbie was and still is his name— dazzled the crowds with his deft moves on the field, where Robbie, the adolescent wonder, reigned supreme. But now, he's a step slower. Wonder how long his run will be."

But, Robbie missed his mom and dad and three sisters especially during the Christmas holidays, when he would be playing far from home. On those occasions, Emma included him in our holiday dinners. I recall her saying for three years straight to our star player, "I know this isn't home, but we will make it as close to home as we can." She knew that all the money could turn a boy into the wrong kind man quickly, so she advised him on financial matters. "You know, Robbie, you've got to pay yourself first." Robbie's reaction remained the same for three years. "So, Mrs. Johnson, just what do you mean by that? I get paid by whoever it is that owns the club."

"You pay yourself when you put money away in a saving or investment account. The owners won't be paying you for a lifetime, you know. Investing some of it gives you the grace of paying yourself when the owners stop paying you." Emma worked as an accountant not only in a midtown office but at home as well. "She's my manager," Danny would repeat. "And she also acts as the unofficial money manager to the younger players on the squad."

Danny reflected on those years, the golden, glory years that had passed by so quickly.

He recalled a line from his schoolboy days, *Fama fugit* "Yes, fame does fly by, too quickly it seems." All those times when he had reviewed films, devised precise drills and scrimmages to prepare for the big games raced through his mind, far faster than even a young Robbie could run. All the games were big and lately, these big losses had stung the crowds, who quickly forgot those three, precious glory years. "All that time I spent coaching, away from Emma and his son and daughter, had come to nought. Dust in the wind, that's what it is, nothing more. No wonder Mark had followed his mother's footsteps and studied finance and accounting. On those increasingly rare visits home, he'd knock the ball about with me, but he wanted nothing more to do with the game. Maybe, when he's a little older, he'll have a child and repeat the drills with her or him, the drills I had taught Mark and Kathleen. Like her older brother, Kathleen, Katie she prefers to be called, dallied with the game, but her heart wasn't in it. No wonder over that. I missed almost all of their youth games. I had put all my energy on my own squad. But, that energy had waned along with the tally of wins.

"The players were making far more money than I was. I suppose the management kept me on as the coach because I was only a minor expense. Now they can't even afford that. Well, I'll quit on my own terms, not wait to be fired. Maybe my daughter Katie can mend some of my arthritic joints, knees and ankles, even my right shoulder. She's in residency now as an orthopedic surgeon, little thanks to me. Emma had kept a trained eye on her daughter's studies while I was off in a futile pursuit of glory. Well, that's all done. Maybe I'll be blessed to have time to make amends, maybe not. Those damning words kept reverberating in my ears, 'A frazzled and feeble and fragile finish—a tragic tinnitus of sorts."

Then Danny stood up, looked around the empty room, then glanced down at the emptied glass, switched on the light and fixed his gaze on the pennants proclaiming past victories. "Well, the past is over and so am I." Then he recalled the words he had told his squads after a crushing defeat "Keep your heads up, lads. You've done your best, and no one can expect any more than that." Sometimes his players believed him—and sometimes not.

"What an ass I am! Here I go, drowning myself in sorrows and pathetic attempts at self pity. It's about time I get to it." He settled down at his laptop; at least it would be his for a few more minutes and typed out his resignation. "There, that should do it. Of course, I've offered to stay on until the new coach is hired, but I've got a feeling that the new coach has already been groomed to replace me. Probably that guy who sits in the stands right above our bench. He keeps tapping away at his laptop furiously through every match. Nothing to do other than to start cleaning out my desk." Danny opened a drawer stuffed with the detritus of years of use: receipts for equipment that had already worn out years ago, paper clips, pencil, pens, sticky notes intended to act as reminders for purchases long forgotten, clippings from newspaper headlines, and other assorted office flotsam and jetsam. "I suppose I ought to tidy up this mess, and let the new guy create his own wreckage. Well, maybe it won't be wreckage. I wish the new coach well."

Then Danny took out his keys to open the file cabinet marked "Confidential." It contained detailed records for each player. Danny thumbed through a few and observed, "It's all computerized now. These paper files date back a decade or more. They have become as outdated as I have become: records of 40 meter sprint times, heights of vertical jumps, runs with the ball and without the ball, fouls committed, goals and assists tallied, minutes played, and some of the subjective assessments of coaches and assistant coaches. It seems as if all we do is judge players, people, everybody on a whole host of standards. I've spent a lifetime judging others; now it's time for others to judge me. So, that's what it is all about: imperfect judgments in an imperfect world that demands perfection." Danny then picked up an armful of files and carried them over to the shredding machine. "Soon to be used as packing for—I don't know— maybe beauty supplies, covering up blemishes."

Behind Danny, Groundskeeper #2, Al Lovington was opening the door. Danny heard the door creak on hinges that had, thirty years ago, swung noiselessly. "Well, so it's you Coach Danny. Preparing for the next match, are you"

"In a manner of speaking, Al, I suppose it's true."

"So, are they sacking you? Words gotten around, you know."

"Not quite. I've beaten them to the knock out punch."

"So, you're dodging the knockout punch then? Well, Coach Danny, we'll miss you; but, when it's time, it's time. Still no shame in that. You've had a grand roller coaster ride, you know like the waves rolling up and down—"

"And then crashing against the shore."

"It's not that, Coach. Fellows come and go in this business. You've stuck around far longer than most. That's something to be proud of. I've been working here for over forty-five years. And, as far as I know, there's none that can beat that record."

"No, I suppose not."

"Well, since it's only you, I've nothing to report. I'll leave you to your memories. Be sure to give my best to the missus. She's a grand, fine lady."

"That she is, Al."

"Well, I'll see you at your retirement party."

"What party? Who could have known.?"

"Well, it was going to happen one way or another anyway. You've chosen the better way."

"No one to second guess my call?"

"Not a one."

"I guess I'm the last to know."

"Now, Coach, before I go, you've got to promise me one thing."

"Sure, Al, what?"

"Don't let it out that I told you about your retirement gala, for a gala it will be."

"Not a soul, not even Morgan."

"I wouldn't hold you to that. You've got to tell someone. You'll burst from thoughts come bounding out of your head. Besides, Morgan won't let anyone know."

"All right, I'll let Morgan in on our little secret."

"Right you are, Danny." Al extended his arm, forearm rippling with all the toil of his forty-five years. Danny shook it with all his strength, but his grip couldn't match Al's. "Now remember. Don't tell anyone except Morgan, not Emma, not Mark, not Katie."

"You've got my word on that."

Al left, once again leaving Danny in silence. He shredded documents for twenty minutes before giving it all up. "I've got to get out in the air or I'll suffocate myself with these mounds of paper."

In mid-January, the skies darkened early. At ten pm, the darkness coated everything; later in the new year, it wouldn't feel so deeply dark until midnight. But, the air had more of a brisk autumnal feel to it. Danny gazed up at the skies. The stars shone brightly against a backdrop of darkness. Some glowed brighter than others. "Al's a good fellow. His son plays right now for a second division club. At Al's insistence, I watched him play one day. He's a decent player—good ball skills and a good head for the game—much the way I was in my playing days. Unfortunately, he lacks the speed to be a topflight player. Of course, I didn't tell Al this. No sense in hurting an old companion. But his son sensed that I was damning him with faint praise—and I was. But, perhaps I should have been more frank. I've known players who have thrown away their youth on a dream that had little likelihood of ever becoming a reality." He walked on a bit farther, perhaps a quarter of a mile. Home lay only another mile away. Danny insisted on having his home close to the vast facility where he spent the bulk of his days. Of course, the stadium rested in its glory, a modern day version of a medieval cathedral, but beyond the stadium sprawled out beyond the car park also lay the training grounds with two fields, one for grass and a smaller one with artificial turf. Then, there were the corporate offices for merchandising, marketing, accounts receivable, accounts payable, all that stuff that Danny would have liked to ignore in his quest for his version of the grail..

As Danny paused and looked up at the skies, he observed for the first time just how many stars he could see. "I guess I amount to one faint star among so many, my light barely visible. But then I'm just one small glimmer among so many. Maybe that's my greatest failing. It's not all about me, is it." Then he reflected on just how many times, he had to tell a young man of nineteen or twenty that the club would have to let him go.Where that young man or so many like him went, Danny didn't know. "Of course, I was wrong a few times, less than a handful. Three went on to achieve their football dreams with another club, but those instances were outweighed by dozens upon dozens more. Well, I got the privilege of living the dream for a while. For that I should be grateful. I just wish I had been just more considerate about what lay beyond the dreams of athletic glory."

As Danny neared home, he also regretted that he had neglected Emma and Mark and Katie as much as he had. "Perhaps, I owe my family the time I spent running after an elusive dream. Just the thought of admitting to them that I had failed, that I resigned rather than face the shame of being fired weighs me down."

His house, actually more of a cottage, blended into the lower middle class neighborhood around it with one exception, a small two stall stable and a three acre plot of fenced yard, where he and Emma would ride

Morgan. Later, Robbie and Katie would ride as well. The second stall had housed a pony when the children were too young to handle Morgan—not that Morgan ever presented a problem. Emma and Danny had bought the horse years ago and named the gelding Morgan for that was his breed. Few others housed Morgans in the county where they lived. So, Morgan, the Morgan, had grown up with the household. Danny would ride the chestnut gelding whenever he could, and Emma had scheduled in a ride at least four times a week. Tonight, though, Danny wouldn't ride his prized Morgan, just walk with him around the pasture. "Well, my friend, I suppose it's time I joined you here. I guess you could say we've both been put out to pasture. Not that you don't have some rides left, you know, some good, long rides." Morgan's large eyes focused on the treats Danny had brought along as he always had on the night of a home match. They rounded the oval patch of the pasture just quietly walking along together, pausing only for Morgan to to nibble on one of the treats. "Well, my friend, it's time for you to get back to your stall for the night. Tomorrow we'll ride early in the morning."

Danny didn't want to cross the threshold of his house any sooner than he could. He dallied about, just standing there, exhaling and thinking to himself, "How can I face Emma?"

He paused and blew out a long breath of resignation before he entered the code, opened the door, and tried to move as softly as a summer breeze. He didn't. Emma stormed in. "Danny, where have you been? Words gotten out, and Mr. Squires wants to talk with you right away, as he said to me, 'Tell Danny to call me as soon as he gets in. I don't care how late it is.'"

"Emma, I was just out walking with Morgan. I stayed later after the game to tidy up the mess of my office space. You've always said that my desk looks like a dumpster pile. All is neat and tidy now almost as tidy as your desk upstairs."

"Danny, out with it. You're just dancing around the truth, aren't you? You've cashed it in, haven't you?"

"Yes," Danny admitted, just easing himself in his worn recliner, trying to avoid eye contact with Emma.

"Well, Danny, it's not as if we haven't all seen this coming."

Danny continued to stare blankly at the floor, but Emma would have none of it. "Look in the mirror, Danny."

He knew what Emma meant but wanted to deflect a truth he couldn't face. "Oh, you mean like,'Mirror, mirror, on the wall, who's the biggest loser of them all?"

"Danny, aren't you a little old to be pouting?"

"You're right, Emma.I know you're right. Maybe I could get on at a different club?" Danny said this half-heartedly. He knew he couldn't. His time had come and gone. Danny kept looking down now at his folded hands, almost as if praying. "Will we have enough to keep Morgan?"

"Danny, you've had a good run, better than most. I've been putting money aside for this ever since you started coaching. Coaching's not the most secure type of business to be in. Yes, we can keep Morgan and do some of the things we've talked about but never done. Maybe take a long road trip places we've never been, taking Morgan with us. And soon enough we'll be grandparents. Have you thought about that? You know that Mark and his wife have been talking about starting a family. Or perhaps you've tuned out those not-so subtle hints they've been dropping. It's time to admit that coaching is a job, a business, and you've made a decent salary doing what you like to do. Not many people get that chance. Now, get on your high horse Morgan and the three of us will ride off into the sunset, laughing all the way—well, maybe not quite, but good enough."

Danny just nodded his head. He knew Emma was right. He got up from his chair slowly, went over and kissed his wife of many years and said matter-of-factly, "I suppose it's time to call Mr. Squires."

"You do that. Then come on up to bed. I've got a pretty fair idea of the gist of what you two will be talking about."

Danny took out his phone, drew a deep breath, and made the call.

"Yes, Danny, I'm glad you called. I suppose you knew what was coming. Still, I don't want to leave you on bad terms. You've made quite a few friends during your tenure, the longest time one coach has ever served. I'll accept your resignation under one condition. In a month, we'll schedule in a farewell bash . That will give us enough time to contact former players and friends. So, precisely four weeks from today we'll have a little fun."

"Do you want me to stay on until then?"

"I think it best you don't—a clean break. We have someone ready to slide into your place. Well, Danny goodby, we'll see you in four weeks." The brusque ending had rattled the old coach's nerves.

Danny had caught himself before he could say: "You mean sneak in. So, you've been planning to replace me for just how long? Maybe after the third game of the season when we we had one win on a disputed call and two losses." But Danny didn't say that. Emma was right: it was a business, nothing more and nothing less, a way to make a living and, perhaps, have a little fun along the way. Still, the whole decision remained hard to stomach, but "that's the way it goes," Danny said out loud, trying to convince himself. "You know the old saying 'The king is dead; long live the king.' For me, the saying goes, 'the coach is gone; long live his replacement.' Well, Emma's right. I need to look at the whole business rationally My heart was in the game more than my brain." He took each step up to his bedroom slowly and deliberately. Emma lay there sleeping. Danny kissed her cheek ever so gently so that she wouldn't wake up. Danny then made his way to the other side of the bed and sat down, reflecting. " You know, it's not all about me after all . The whole business has been hard on her, too. She always took it on herself to advise the young players. A few brushed her off, but the majority welcomed a little bit of mothering. Besides, he glanced over at Emma, noticing the her once raven hair was being replaced by white. "We're both getting old. Emma was planning on retiring in another year or two. Then, maybe, and maybe before then, we can take those trips Emma mentioned. Meanwhile, perhaps I can do a little mothering for her."

Danny couldn't sleep, so he got up early and made his version of a grand breakfast for the two of them: omelettes, sausage, biscuits dripping with honey, fresh strawberries lying resplendent in whipped cream. When Emma came down, her eyes opened at the sight. "Danny, you've outdone yourself. But don't be doing this every morning or we'll grow fatter and fatter. You don't want to be so heavy that you can't ride Morgan, you know."

"Don't worry, Emma. I just couldn't sleep, and cooking kept my mind from churning over the same regrets over and over. This will do for both breakfast and lunch."

"Danny, I've got to go or I'll be late. Off to work. We'll talk about my work later." They exchanged a brief kiss. Then Emma advised, "Take Morgan for a spin. You both would profit from the exercise. And, after today's breakfast you will need to burn some calories."

As soon as Emma left, Danny cleaned up the kitchen, grabbed a carrot for Morgan, and headed over to the barn. Morgan awaited him there, eyeing the carrot ravenously. Danny suspected that Morgan knew that the carrot was a bribe. "Danny would be saddling me soon," so the horse seemed to think. "Then we'll go out for a gentle ride."

Morgan resigned himself to his fate. "Humans were a strange lot," so seemed to think Morgan. "Well, here we go for the humbug ride of a slow walk."

But Morgan had guessed wrong. The two started out on a slow walk, but then the walk turned to a trot, the trot turned into a canter, and then for ten glorious seconds, a full gallop. Danny leaned forward in the saddle so that only inches separated his head from the horse's. Morgan's black mane encircled Danny, and for a brief spell, the two appeared as one. Then the gallop descended into a canter, then a trot, then a slow walk. Danny dismounted about thirty yards from the stable and then strode side by side with Morgan. The morning sun seemed to hover over Morgan's head, crowning it. The two entered the stable, where Danny removed saddle, reins, and all traces of human control. Then he fetched one of the biscuits, he stored in a small cabinet. "Here, Morgan, you can revel in a morning feast, too—not every morning, but this morning." Morgan took the biscuit from Danny's stretched palm and ground it slowly. Then, out of habit, the horse turned towards his stall, but Danny had other thoughts. "No, Morgan run free in the pasture if you like."

As Danny walked back home, he paused after thirty yards and turned to face Morgan. Then the two locked eyes as if sharing the same soul. The Morgan turned and trotted off to the far end of the field and Danny strode home.

In four weeks, Danny had his retirement party. He and Emma mingled with former players along with Al Lovingston and all the groundskeepers. Most of the conversation centered on commonplace matters: how are you, how are your family, what will you do in retirement, keep in touch, and matters like that. But Danny encountered two discussions he would treasure.

Al's son approached Danny somewhat nervously. Danny feared the worst, some exchange like, "Well, I showed you, you bastard." But the young man paused in front of Danny and blurted out, "You were right, Coach, I mean about my career as a footballer and all. Now I've got a job, a good one, nothing spectacular, but it pays the bills, and I'm getting married soon. Will you come to my wedding?"

"I'd be honored," Danny replied. Then Emma took the youth in hand and rained down a hundred questions about his future wife and the ceremony, and all the details that Danny gladly handed over to her.

The next person who faced Danny approached him like an old friend, extending his hand. "No hard feelings, Danny. We sportscasters tend to overdramatize things a bit, so all that business about you having a frazzled, feeble, and fragile finish. Well, that was part of the game. You know that the crowd loves it. But don't worry, I've got new headlines for you, that run like this: 'Retired, Relaxed, Rejuvenated, and Renowned.' How do you like that?"

"It's all part of the game, isn't it?"

Yes," the announcer grinned. "I'm glad you finally figured it all out."

ON THE CUSP OF IT ALL

"What is hell? Hell is oneself."

—T. S. Eliot

"Hell is other people."

—Jean-Paul Sartre

"Hell is empty and all the devils are here."

—William Shakespeare

"There is no greater hell than to be a prisoner of fear."

—Ben Jonson

A Few Final Considerations

Slicing up cucumbers, peppers, tomatoes, and some romaine lettuce for a light dinner, I eased into my evening routine: preparing a meal, greeting my wife with an almost perfunctory kiss, engaging in a little conversation about the somewhat banal details of the workday routine, the same-old, same-old. Mary, my life partner (we used to say spouse or even wife, but times have changed) scoured the mail for the bills that came with the end of the month. She called it the end-times. To alleviate the tedium, I clicked up the volume of the TV news. I never really watched much of the news, just listened to detached voices droning on about the same-old, same-old with occasional loud rants by politicians. After a while, it all blends into background music—a repetitive droning interrupted by the jarring clash of political cymbals. But listening isn't quite as annoying as watching would be. I don't mind missing the pasted on smiles of the anchors anyway. While I listened to the litany of murders, robberies, rising prices, and predictions about the weather and the next football game, I continued with my repetitive chop-chops.

But then a scream roared out of the TV, "Lord Jesus, help us." This distressed cry could have referred to the latest random drive-by shooting, the sky high increase in rents that would certainly throw more people out onto the streets, the corrupt politicians who had taken yet another bribe, or sundry other calamities—so many, in fact, that most of us had grown numb to the seemingly endless river of violence greed, and corruption that threatened to drown us all—even people like me who had taken refuge in the safety of our homes, an illusion like a thin veneer of ice coating an isolated pool of deadly waters, at once so serene and so malevolent. "Lord Jesus, help us," indeed. We're all skating on thin ice.

Mary took a few bites from the plate that lay in front of her. "Looks as if we'll have to cut back even more on our grocery bill—either that or dip into our modest savings. Still, we have something to eat. There's a lot of people worse off."

"I don't know, Mary, some people must be raking in the big bucks. They're building more and more of those half a million or more dollar homes. I don't think we could even afford to pay the real estate taxes on some of the McMansions."

"Yeah, Pete, at the same time those tent cities are springing up in the parks where the kids used to play soccer. And I don't think that one port-a-potty can service eighty or more campers. The invisible poor aren't as invisible as they used to be."

We cleaned up the dishes. As I silently placed the dishes into the dishwasher, I entertained a quite unoriginal digression. "Why do we say cleaned *up* or listen *up* or, in my case screw *up*? U P—do I pee up or down or all around?" Neither original nor profound, my thoughts drifted here and there as if I were vainly trying to keep myself from doing anything worthwhile or thinking anything of substance. I suppose I was growing meaninglessly monotonous like the voices on the TV. I had degenerated into the very insipid, sophomoric thoughts that I claimed to abhor.

"A penny for your thoughts, Pete."

"They're not worth that much."

"So, you're basically telling me to mind my own business."

"I didn't mean it that way. I don't know. My mind's a foggy mess right now. I feel lost and rudderless on some river that's drifting to no place in particular."

"Now that the kids are grown and on their own, I know what you mean. When we were younger and had no time to think, we yearned for the freedom for our minds to wander. Now, we wander but don't know where we're going.

"Well, in the short term, I know where I'm going. I'm headed to bed even if it's only eight o'clock."

"So, to paraphrase you, you're essentially telling me that I should mind my own business."

"No, Mary, I'm just tired in mind and body and soul, just worn out. I'll probably feel better in the morning.

"Well, pleasant dreams, Pete. I'll join you in a little while after I finish cleaning the floor.

With that, I trudged upstairs to bed. Drunk. Blottoed. Wasted. I hadn't even had a drink, but I kept bumping into things—like the bathroom door I just banged into. Wandering aimlessly in the miasma of my mind. I must be just some kind of self-centered, sixty something adolescent. Eight o'clock. What did Poor Richard say, "Early to bed and early to rise makes a man healthy, wealthy, and wise"? Early to bed means I'll wake up at four am, eyes wide open and stomach growling, and mind still wandering around aimlessly. I heard that old Ben himself never followed the advice of Poor Richard; he just frolicked about in the luxury of the French court, a natural man in a most unnatural place. With that, my mind transported me back over two centuries ago to the bewigged world of the powdered and perfumed aristocrats, hermetically sealed off from the maddening crowd outside. Soon they would be dragged off from the palace to the guillotine with matted hair lying in a pool of blood.

"Snap out of it, old Pete. You're making me sick, and it takes a lot to make my stomach churn."

"What!? Who's there?" I shouted but only in my mind. My body lay motionless on the bed. Not even my lips parted. Still I spoke but no sounds came from my mouth.

"Pete, you're taking yourself way too seriously. Look around, there's a gorilla in the room."

"What are you talking about? Who are you? I don't see anything?"

"Of course, you don't. Your eyes are closed. Unlock that prison cell of a brain you have and look about. Then tell me what you see."

Exhaling slowly, I stepped out of my thoughts and opened my eyes and beheld—"What? There's a six hundred and fifty pound gorilla at the foot of my bed!"

"Take it easy, Pete. You'll scare Mary. She's busy now, escaping her own web of confusion by throwing herself into cleaning. That trick works for a little while. You know the intoxication of frenzied work. She'll be up in a little while, but, only after you and I have a little chat."

"About what?"

"You'll see, but first let me introduce myself. I'm Phil, Phil the Gorilla. I knew your dad well. He used to visit me as often as he could. He was a pretty good guy for a human. He never teased or tormented me. By gazing into his eyes, I knew he felt sorry for me all locked up in the grey concrete of the old-time zoological exhibition room. It was a weird place, part prison, part exhibition room, as if the animals were paintings or mummies or something in a museum or, even worse, lifer-prisoners in a maximum security cell. I hear from my gorilla friends that things are better now. No steel bars. No, the animals—that is, other than the humans—can cavort about in natural dirt and trees and stuff like that. Oh, it's still an exhibition room with some kind of super-strength glass instead of steel bars, but it's all a lot less prison than it used to be. Anyway, I digress.I've been assigned a mission-"

"Wait a minute, Phil. You're telling me that you're the ghost of the big silver back gorilla that my father talked about, the one at the zoo?"

"Well, you got that right."

"What's this about a mission?"

"First off, you've got to understand that I'm not some type of Halloween ghost. I'm more of an angel, I guess—although don't tell Archangel Michael that. He's a stickler for hierarchical order, you know. Anyway, I don't go around scaring people. I'm more like a spiritual therapist, I guess. Only my patients don't come to me. I come to them and generally when they least expect me to. Anyway, you're a guy, a human, who certainly needs some talking to. I mean what"'s with all this maudlin stuff. You think you've got it bad. Well, you don't. You think life is hell? Well, I'm going to give you a taste of hell all right"

"What are you going to do to me?"

"Hey, easy, man, easy. I didn't mean a taste of hell like I was going to beat you up or anything. No, I'm going to be you tour guide to hell and to a few other places. I'll give you a sample of what real hell is."

"Go on—as long as you're not going to beat me up or send lightning bolts from above to kill me."

"Naw, I wouldn't do that. In the afterlife—if you make it there as an animal—all the creatures live in peace. You know, the lion lies down with the lamb and stuff like that. But, don't get me wrong. I mean traces of the old divisions remain.Like, for instance, when I'm escorting a soul through hell, I'll talk about the Leopard of Malice and Fraud. But, if a leopard were doing the escorting, that being would talk about, say, the Monkey of Malice and Fraud. I'll be talking about the Lion of Violence and Ambition; but, if a lion was the escort, it would be the Gorilla of Violence and Ambition. And, I hate to admit it, but I've done more than my fair share of chest thumping if you know what I mean. And, then there's the Wolf of Incontinence, which I prefer to call the Wolf of Excess—too much food, too much drink, too much sex. So, Pete, if you were me, what would you substitute for Wolf?"

"I guess I'd say raccoon—the kind that stuffs his gullet with all kinds of garbage."

"Good choice, Pete. We're in sync, first cousins you might say. Now, I've got to admit that sometimes during my earthly days I'd get a little violent, you know ticked off, at those who taunted me, the idiots who felt safe as long as those steel bars stood between me and them. Those jerks would jump up and down and try to make ape noises and scratch their sides. Most of the time, I ignored the idiots, but not always. Sometimes I'd get even by slyly sneaking over to the pool that lay just inside my cage. And, when the taunters were jumping up, I'd splash the idiots with water. So, sometimes I'd get a little edgy. And, I've got to admit that I really craved that Budweiser at the end of the day. My human keeper would open up a cold glass bottle, drink half of it and then let me have the rest.

Ah, that frothy foam just eased its way down my throat— Wait, you don't believe me?"

"It's just that I never thought some emissary from above would drink beer."

"Well, I do, not too much, just a little half bottle or even an entire bottle. Say, have you got a cold one down in your fridge?"

"Yeah, Phil, go get yourself one" I watched Phil disappear just as quickly as he had come. "What's going on with me? I'm talking to a gorilla, a dead one at that, as if he were some long lost friend. Have I lost my mind?"

"You recycle glass, don't you?" Phil asked in an offhand way as if he were a buddy who had just stopped by. His enormous hairy hand wrapped itself around the bottle as if it were his security blanket, firmly but gently at the same time.

"Yeah, Phil, the recycling bin is in the garage."

"I'll take care of it when I finish. I like to sip it slowly, you know, just to prolong the pleasure. In fact, that's one of the reasons I volunteer for these jobs back on earth. I get a few beers, and a reminder that I've got it pretty good in the afterlife. For humans and animals, life can be tough. When I come down here, I don't like seeing beer cans strewn about. They've got their place. Far sadder than that sight, though, is the vision of some poor 'possum or deer smashed flat against the concrete. We've all got to die, but we're not garbage. You know I remember a line from ole Joseph Heller, "The spirit gone, man is garbage.' In a lot of respects, we're all garbage—human and animal alike—but it's the spirit, the soul that makes the difference. But I digress—"

Phil shot a look amazement and consternation. "What, you think that I can't read? Well, I can. One of the first things I did in the afterlife was to learn how to read. I hated to admit it, but some humans have some great ideas. Yeah, but the first step in my mission is to show you the hell of those humans who have either lost any trace of their humanity and so are consigned to the hell of their being. Here, take my hand, we're headed down, down to the bowels of the earth, where flames burn and rocks melt."

Without thinking, I did what Phil asked. He didn't order me, but I felt I couldn't refuse. We flew out the window and plunged down some volcano—Mount Vesuvius maybe. At least, I like to think so. And there we stood at the gates of hell.

"Aw, hell, here we go again," a lesser devil limped his way over all the while trying to shoo away the mass of flies that by buzzed around his head. A stack of keys hung round his midsection and clanged and clanged and clanged in the most jarring way. Other lesser devils scurried about and banged into each other and cursed each other and us. They made a raucous screeching noise, like a million crows cawing about—pandemonium personified. The acrid smell of sulphur hung about him like a thundercloud. "So, Phil, you on escort service again? Trying to make me feel bad by seeing how good you got it? Yeah, well, you're an SOB all right, and I hate you for it. I hate that puny human you got with you, too. What a pathetic sight. Yeah, well, I like it here—the stink, the flames, the screams, the whole shebang, so don't try to lord it over me. I 'm an SOB, and I like it that way. So there, you pair of goody two-shoes. Yeah, yeah, yeah, I'll open the damn gates, just leave me the hell alone, will ya."

Phil turned his head towards me and shook it gently, his eyes opened wide. His expression seemed to saying, "Yeah, this is it, the same old hell—petty, pernicious, and putrid."

"So, I guess you two bastards want to see the very depths of hell first, right? Go one, you SOB's. Phil knows the way. I hate the two of you. Maybe I'll see the human guy in a little while. Sweet dreams, you two pricks."

We descended down and down, a seeming eternity of plunging, only to find ourselves surrounded by masses of burning, churning lava that swirled about us. "Pete, don't worry. That lava won't touch us. I've got a VIP card / Guest Pass that keeps us immune from the worst punishments, but you will feel a little heat and you might even break out into a sweat. You'll sniff that sulfuric stench. I mean, otherwise, it wouldn't really be hell, right?"

"I guess not," I reluctantly replied. It was getting hot and sweat began breaking out from my pores and my nose contorted itself as I vainly tried to block out the stench.

"Pete, I'm not saying you'll get used to it. No one does. In a little while, though, your body will adjust and you'll be able to tolerate it all. I've got to add that you'll have to take a break from all the heat and malodorous fumes. After prolonged exposure, it really gets to you.When we leave hell—which won't be for a while—we'll get a cleaning shower. For now, though, we'll have to grin and bear it. We're headed to the depths of hell where dwell the souls of those condemned for malice and fraud. Wait! Stop for a minute. There you see the Leopard-devil sneaking about in the flames, disguised among the smoke and fame, the miasma of the lowest depths of hell. Soon he'll be out of sight, only to reappear again, ever vigilant to bring back fugitives to their fate. I've read Dante, you know. Now, I'm not bragging or anything; but, when I finish this mission, old Dante and I will have a sit down discussion about how hell has changed over the centuries."

Then Phil strained his eyes and then covered his brow with his enormous right hand to better spy some shadowy form lurking in dark shadows. "But look ahead, past the smoke and flames. What do you see?"

Phil still stood there gazing at that dark, mysterious form that lay in the shadows, poised to strike. I glanced at Phil and then directed my focus to that distant figure and then answered Phil's question: "I see a large cat-like creature slowly loping through the dense jungle of shadows and half-shadows, Phil. He or she or whatever seems ready to pounce upon some unsuspecting prey."

"That would be the Leopard of Malice and Fraud. The worst of the frauds would be those posing as ministers of God, those who preach solely for their own profit and advantage. Dante described how the simoniacs were thrust head down in a a hole with their exposed feet being scorched with flames. A just punishment for those who have turned their spiritual mission upside down, and made money and sex their goals rather than salvation. Well, times have changed, and there's a vulgar expression that goes, 'They've got their head up their ass.' Well, that's what happens here. Those who preach the virtues of humility and charity but live a life of arrogance and luxury have turned religion on its head. They've got their heads up their asses, and so they have their just deserts."

And so they do. I saw a prominent televangelist who lived in a palatial mansion, forty-nine rooms and more, on a forty acre compound, complete with a landing strip for his private jet, a swimming pool, and tennis court to relieve the stress of preaching what he didn't believe, and more. He always sported tailored suits and argued to himself that, as one bringing salvation to all, he must look divine. He whisked about the country on his private jet, dubbed the Angel of the Lord. Now he stands, naked and contorted in that vile pose Phil had discussed, inhaling his own filth.

98

Taking in this panorama of pain, I spied a mitered bishop bent over with his emblem of office stuck up his hole. He shot me an envious look and I felt ashamed and fearful. In life, he had preached that greed was the root of all evil. Now, he truly knew it was. He had his bishop's house redesigned five times during his fifteen year tenure, adding one more creature comfort after another. It was rumored that he dined only on beef tenderloin except during Lent, when he feasted on lobster and shrimp. He had his episcopal robes made by the finest (and most expensive) tailor in the Western world. Now, stained with his own filth, they had degenerated into tattered and foul rags.

Then to the right of his eminence, stood a rabbi, famous for his learning and for his ability to relieve rich widows of the burden of their wealth. Here he had no one left to woo. All he could do was to bemoan his fate.

Scanning over these scenes of wretchedness, I beheld an iman, who had in his lifetime married five fifteen-year-old virgins, besides—it was rumored—a like number of concubines. He had locked up all of his brides in private rooms for his private pleasures.

Sickened by what I had seen, I begged Phil to take me out of this damned place. Nodding his head in affirmation, he quietly took me back to my bed but only after we had luxuriated in that cleansing shower he had talked about.

I woke up, screaming. "It was a dream, wasn't it Wasn't it? I mean hell is only a theological construct—maybe an outdated one at that. Or, hell is other people. Isn't that the way it goes? Or, maybe it's like hell is oneself, right? Or I remember something like hell is empty and all the devils are here, I don't know. I don't know. I just don't know."

"Pete, Pete, wake up! You've drenched yourself and the sheets in sweat. At least I hope it's sweat."

"Mary, I don't know."

"You don't know what, Pete?"

"I don't know. I just feel as if I'm on the cusp of it all."

"You're not going to die on me, Pete, are you?" Mary's eyes betrayed bemusement, fear, incredulity, and all at the same time. "Go take a shower, Pete. Are you sick to your stomach?"

"No, not sick to the stomach. I'll go take that shower," but I felt a bewildering sense of deja vu.

While Mary changed the sheets, I took that shower. And, for some reason, poured myself a glass of Budweiser—but only half of the can. I left the other half in the can and set it on the kitchen counter.

In a short while, I went back to the bed and back to sleep.

How long I slept I don't know, but midway through a deep sleep, I felt a nudge, and one from a hairy hand. "Phil, is that you?"

"None other, and, oh, thanks for leaving me that half can of Bud. It reminds me of the old days."

"Yeah, sure, no problem."

"I've been thinking it over and it just wouldn't be fair to leave you with only that glimpse of hell. You got to see the other side, too."

"The other side? You mean heaven?"

"Well, I can't show you heaven. It'd be just too much. But, I can show you this." Phil extended his powerful arm and pointed to a pathway that wound its way around a huge mountain. Beyond that mountain a gleaming light shone on, and all these pilgrim souls were walking toward that light. "I can't really explain it, but Dante gave us a glimpse of it all:

The glory of Him who moves all things rays forth
through all the universe, and is reflected
from each thing in proportion to its worth.
I have been in the Heaven of His most light,
And what I saw, those who descend from there
lack both the knowledge and the power to write.

Then, I awoke again, but this time not screaming. Mary still lay there undisturbed. I softly rose and turned on every light in the downstairs. "No, this isn't it. That light had a gleam to it. "Oh, who am I kidding. I was just dreaming, wasn't I? What a fool I am." But, I eased over to the kitchen counter. There stood that can of beer—but it was empty and scrawled in marker on the top of the can was a one word message that read only this, "Thanks."

I was, indeed, on the cusp of it all—knowledge and ignorance, foolishness and wisdom, light and dark, human and animal, body and soul, life and whatever comes after life.